Diabla

Alyx Gaudio

ISBN: 9798640501698

CONTENTS

ACKNOWLEDGEMENTS

Addiction is the evil paramour of the most gifted souls. It masquerades as part of the creative process but slowly destroys genuine talent, catapulting the artist into irrepressible depression. Addiction forces the mind to go to war with itself. I would like to devote this book to a friend of mine who was a victim of this cycle. A creative mind with extraordinary talent that passed away too young.
RIP Jiffy…

ADOLESCENCE

My neighbor stands gracelessly on the corner, watching the school kids get on the bus. He has no children but loves to be around them in his coffee-stained tattered robe and sockless slippers. He proclaims he's not a stranger amongst the neighborhood children, though it makes me feel stranger than a twelve-year-old should ever feel.

This is the person who is still free—the one who meanders around my cul-de-sac, preying on whomever he desires. "He lays on me," I say to my seventh-grade guidance counselor. She blinks twice and takes a breath.

"What do you mean he lays on you?" she asks, leaning forward in her off-kilter swivel chair. I shrug vacantly as the familiar feeling of numbness takes over.

"Until his thing finishes," I stutter, shifting my glance to the clock above her desk. Mrs. Holloway shakes her head in total abhorrence of my allegation and changes the expression on her face for my benefit.

"Domenica, this is a very serious accusation. I need to speak with Officer Bronson. Are you okay to wait in my office for a few minutes?"

"Am I in trouble?"

"Of course not," Mrs. Holloway declares, taken aback by my question.

"He said it was illegal for both of us."

"That's what predators say so they can keep hurting you. I'll make sure he can never go near you again," Mrs. Holloway says before storming out of her office.

It's a nice thought, sure. I know she doesn't have the power to make something like that happen. Even if my school resource officer gets Mr. Carson in trouble, the memory of him will still haunt me.

I've gotten good at blocking the bad parts from my memory, but I can't always do it. He comes and goes when he pleases. After what seems like an eternity, Mrs. Holloway returns to her office. She catches me staring at the pictures on her desk.

"Domenica—"

"Are these your kiddos?" I ask, shifting my gaze from one frame to the next. She nods patiently, understanding the delicate state of my psyche wants nothing more than to deflect from the situation at hand.

"How old are they?"

"Nineteen and twenty-three," Mrs. Holloway says as I pick up the second picture frame. I stop my pointless pursuit of questions and put the picture down, giving her my full attention.

"Sweetie, I have to ask you a very difficult question." Mrs. Holloway takes her time before continuing, surveying my composure with meticulous execution. "When was the last time he laid on you?"

"Yesterday," I reply in my shrill twelve-year-old voice.

"Okay, here's what's going to happen next. I'm going to call your mom to the school so she can take you to the hospital with the police. They're going to collect DNA from you so they can put this man in jail today. Does that make sense?"

"Yes," I reply, feeling the weight of the situation intensify as I try to comprehend that I've done nothing wrong. *I was manipulated by someone smarter than me, who took advantage. He wants me to be afraid. I hate this feeling.*

Mrs. Holloway exits to speak with Officer Bronson again. I wait in her office for what feels like an hour, then suddenly become startled by the blood-curdling scream of my mother receiving the news in the hallway. The door quickly flings open, and she rushes in to hug me.

The resource officer and a detective follow behind, probably to ensure she doesn't leave the school to hurt Mr. Carson.

My mother expresses several things while clinging onto me, though it's hard to decipher the exact words because she's so distraught. "We'll give you two a moment."

"Mom, I'm okay," I say quietly. This only makes her cry harder, though. The impassiveness my voice carries with it is enough to motivate the detached detective to step out of the room. It even makes *me* want to break down. But the subconscious scab blocks tears from ever beginning to form.

I shift my look to Officer Bronson. His eyes are dry, with his composure well kept. Clearly, these cops have been faced with pure unadulterated malevolence once or twice before. The crime rate in American Falls is shockingly oversaturated for a small town. Mostly drug-related assaults, domestic disputes, and the occasional homicide here and there.

The reason I can't cry is because I feel nothing. Randy Carson already snatched my feelings from me three years ago, after the first time it happened. All I have left is my aptitude to observe. My capacity to remain calm within this fucked-up, chaotic situation seemingly impresses the cops.

The hospital personnel bombards us with questions while poking and prodding me like I'm some adolescent lab rat. They all keep repeating the phrase, "we're so sorry," repeatedly—as if them apologizing for my neighbor's actions can make up for what this person has done.

The worst part isn't that it happened once a week; it's the fact that I allowed it to. A part of me knew he was a bad man. He was so good at persuasion until I realized my body had every modicum of power over his proclivity. It was only very recently when this came about. As soon as that clicked, I knew I could stop him.

The detective enters with one of the nurses. My mother tightens her grip around my hand as they approach. "We have enough evidence to make the arrest." My mother stands and hugs both. She looks back at me. Still, I feel nothing. Just by speaking up, I've already won. Whether he's in jail or not, the concrete realization that I can hurt anyone who hurts me first solidifies.

Mr. Carson is sentenced to ten years behind bars, a length of time that I believe to be too generous for such an awful human being. My middle school years to follow are nothing short of exhilarating. Boys, boys, and more boys. By the time I'm a sophomore, I start to experiment with girls. I can't seem to get enough.

My hormones grow additionally erratic with each birthday that passes. I have more intercourse in my high school years than Charlie Sheen probably had in his pre-HIV days. Every guy on the football team knows me by the birthmark on my lower back. And every cheerleader in school wants nothing to do with me. These girls hate how I can do more with the tip of my tongue than all twenty of them can do with their Kegels.

I don't know what the psychology is behind my desire to be defiled by strangers. My state-funded counselor says it has something to do with what happened with Mr. Carson. I think that could all be bullshit, though. It hasn't necessarily contributed to the most righteous path, though it ensures my ability to always be in control.

By the time I'm twenty, I'm faced with the decision to end my scholastic career as a straight F student, repeating grades multiple times. I could always persuade the Pocatello community college board members to allow me to attend via FAFSA loans. *Sort of seems like a waste of time. Pocatello is the taint-end of America, being the fifth largest meth hub in the country.*

I don't feel like the education I've received from lectures can teach me the most important thing in life, which is how to make money. School is designed for those who follow the rules, and I'm a natural-born dissident.

I break every law the system preaches by doing the exact opposite, which is how I ended up with four thousand dollars in my purse. People who follow the system may have financial security in the long run but find themselves buried with student loans they can never pay back. As for me, I'd rather be cash-rich right fucking now.

"When can I see you again?" The trucker asks, zipping his pants up in the rest stop bathroom stall.

"Long haul or local?"

"I pass through Pokey often enough." He shoots me a mind-mutilating smirk that would make any woman want to run away. Not me, though. My little sheet of meth-covered tin foil on the toilet takes away all fear and replaces it with domination.

"Often enough for what?" I ask while doing another hot rail.

"For a stall fuck," the trucker distastefully mutters. I try not to take what he says personally but fail to choke back my rebuttal.

"Get the fuck out," I reply.

"What if I want my seven hundred back?" His demeanor changes, obviously the pro bono hot rail at the beginning of our session has given him crystal courage. It's not uncommon with these long-haul savants. I pause momentarily, full well knowing if he tries anything stupid, he'll get the shit kicked out of him, and then some.

"I ain't gonna ask you again," I say, standing from my knees to match his intensity.

"Travel stop cum-dump," he utters while pulling a fistful of my hair. The latch quickly flies open. My handler, Sergio, enters, cornering this scrawny fuck dead in his tracks. Sergio slams him against the stall.

"The lady asked you to bounce," Sergio says, surveying the piece of shit's unbuttoned stance.

"What are you, her pimp?"

Sergio sticks his pistol to the trucker's cheek. "Open your wallet."

"She's got her money on the toilet." The trucker becomes aggressive with his tone.

"You want to die, cabrón?" Sergio asks, checking behind

him to ensure our other amigo, Arañato, covers the door.

"Wallet's in the truck."

"Bullshit." Sergio's ruthless side takes over as he snatches the trucker's wallet out of his back pocket, and rummages through his ID and credit cards. "Wendover, huh?" Sergio hands Arañato the man's commercial trucking license.

"I ain't got more cash."

"You got plastic, though." Sergio surveys the numbers on the Amex card.

"You make one purchase on my card and Amex will be so far up your shithouse you won't know up from down inside the pen." The trucker puffs up, clearly unaware of the imminent danger he's in just by opening his mouth. Sergio shares a look with Arañato. All three of us can't help but gawk at his shoddy attempt to back us off.

"I was goin' to let you walk, but I think I just changed my mind." Sergio nods for me to leave the stall so he can deal with this creep accordingly. Arañato opens the door for me on my way out.

The crimson sunset consumes the Pocatello sky as I head back to my Volkswagen behind the rest stop and pack another bowl in the car. I've smoked enough crystal meth to kill three horses. Hand trembles, stammered speech, and paranoia make for the ultimate mind-fuck trifecta. *I don't give a shit, though.* I slept two nights ago.

A Doritos truck pulls into the rest area next to my vehicle.

An older man exits and makes his way towards the travel stop bathroom. I get out and holler at him before he can go in.

"Sorry?" The man replies, holding his hand to his ear for me to repeat what I just said.

"It's occupied," I mutter, taking a few strides closer to him. The Doritos truck driver tries to explain it's an emergency, and there are plenty of stalls. I ask him not to go in again. The way I ask makes him suspicious. He picks up on my amphetamine-induced jaw spasms.

"You high or what?" He asks, taking a closer look.

"Find another rest stop," I demand, now only about five feet from his stance. He shakes his head, not at all entertaining the idea of taking orders from me. He reaches for the handle to go in. As he does, I hit him across the back of the head with a closed fist.

My eyes immediately widen as his face slams into the door frame. I strike him again, knocking the man completely unconscious. The door opens. Sergio and Arañato rush outside to pull me off the innocent Doritos truck driver.

"The fuck is wrong with you, flaca loca?"

"This old ass motherfucker wouldn't back the fuck off," I respond astutely, fidgeting to get situated.

"Let's go!" Sergio drags me back to the car and forces me into the backseat. Arañato grabs the keys out of my purse and starts the car. He shifts in reverse as Sergio climbs in the back next to me and slams the door.

I look over my shoulder, paranoid by all possible outcomes. "Rapido," Sergio yells at the top of his lungs. Arañato backs out and merges onto the 86 towards Chubbuck.

"Fuckin dumbass uneducated motherfuckers," I murmur. My outspoken sentence was only meant to be a thought. That's the problem with crystal meth. Thoughts become words, and words become actions. I try not to skitz-out while we're on the road but can't help myself. This drug has hijacked the frontal cortex, forcing me to utter complete negativity.

"You trying to get us caught or what, bitch?" Sergio asks while taking a shot of his needle on the freeway.

"No, but you ain't doing shit to weed out stupid ass clientele," I say under my breath, trying to comprehend what the fuck I just did. Sergio holds my hand, trying to calm me down.

"You did what you had to do, D," he says in a more relaxed tone. I look to him for a moment, then shift my attention back to the road.

"I got some Xanax back at the room," Arañato mutters while surveying my glance through the rearview mirror.

"Good, I need some," I reply speedily. Arañato smiles and wipes a bead of sweat from his forehead.

As we arrive at the motel in Chubbuck, a feeling of relief

sweeps over me. Somehow, the sight of the dingy Cottontree Inn brings a sense of calmness to my over-tired body. Sergio opens the door and leads us back to the room. Arañato closes the door behind us and rummages through his suitcase on the floor to find his prescription meds.

I take my jacket off and head for the bathroom. I turn on the fan and stare at myself in the mirror. *Holy fuckballs, I look like hell. Bags under my eyes and shit.* After removing my clothes, I jump in the shower, desperate to wash off the five loads I had to endure today. The warm water feels good on my skin.

I reach out of the shower and grab a clean washrag off the towel rack. *Goddamn it. I just realized I used a condom with only two of the guys today. If I catch chlamydia again, I'm going to be pissed.*

I promptly finish my shower and head back into the room. Arañato is passed out on one of the beds with a prescription bottle of Xanax in his hand. Sergio stares out the window, paranoid as fuck. "Stop with that," I utter while digging through my suitcase for a clean pair of panties.

Sergio closes the curtains and takes in the sight of my boney, ass-naked body. He takes one last hit of the pipe and wraps it in a dirty towel off the floor. Sergio smashes the pipe with his boot and dumps the broken glass into the toilet. I finish putting on my bra and feel his cold hands grab my waist from behind.

"No more bomb tonight," I say to him while reaching back to touch his cheek. He kisses me on the neck and proceeds to finger me. I smile, then move his hand away. "I need sleep."

Sergio nods and backs off. He respects me turning him down. The effects crystal meth has on a person's libido is senseless. *Evil actually.* It makes men so fucking horny, yet they can never keep it up. As if fucking the devil's limp dick isn't bad enough, what's worse is they can never cum. *Literally, all I want to do is sleep.*

Sergio grabs the prescription bottle of Xanax and breaks a bar in half for us to split. I have a hard time swallowing it from the cottonmouth and stick my head under the sink to finish washing it down. Sergio turns on the TV and lies in bed. I lie with him, prompting Sergio to take off his boots and get under the covers with me.

He wraps his arms around my body. I gently cuddle into his embrace. *Even though he's a banger, I feel fucking safe with him. Maybe being as connected as he is puts my mind at ease.* Nobody can really touch us, except the cops. Even if we got busted, the money his crew generates is plenty enough for lawyers and bailout fees. My mind begins to quiet as the Xanax kicks in. I kiss Sergio gently on the lips and drift into the much-needed realm of sleep.

I awake the next morning to the sound of banging on the door. Arañato jumps out of bed and looks through the peephole.

"Housekeeping," a soft voice murmurs. Arañato cracks the door and tells the housekeeper to come back in an hour. He slams the door and shakes his head, annoyed the bitch woke him up. "Goddamn, it's already twelve," Sergio utters, surveying the alarm clock on the dresser. I crawl out of bed and put my jeans on.

"You guys headed back to Salt Lake?" I ask while putting my socks and shoes on. Sergio nods and climbs out of bed. Arañato counts the stacks of money on the dresser and bands them up. The stacks surpass the fucking thickness of the hotel room Bible.

The room phone rings. Sergio quickly answers. "Hello?" Sergio pauses for a moment to listen. "Don't be chargin' us for a fuckin extra night. I'm gonna dispute them charges if you do, bitch." Sergio hangs up and catches Arañato's look.

"That's some bullshit," Arañato says, breaking me off my five thousand dollars. I put the money in my purse and throw on a sriracha-stained blouse. Arañato hands Sergio his cut, which appears to be much more than mine. I don't make a fuss about it, though. They covered the room for the two weeks we've been out here.

"Tell Emm when she's done giving it up for free to come down to Salt Lake," Arañato says with a smirk. Sergio shares a laugh with him. For me, it's not funny. Emma's been hooked on this shit since she was fourteen. They've only met her once. I got her to come with me on a string of outcalls for a couple of days. She ended up fucking a John in exchange for a clean Walgreens needle.

I don't consider his comment smirk-worthy whatsoever. My demeanor changes, and I lose my shit a little. "Show some fucking respect," I reply inhospitably. Arañato laughs at my response. I impulsively slap him across the face. He lunges forward and wraps his hands around my throat.

Sergio manages to pull him off and slams him into the wall. "Cálmate!" Sergio yells, looking back at me to make sure I'm okay.

"Come at me improper again, and I'll fuckin kill you," Arañato threatens as Sergio restrains him.

"Try it, you piece of shit!" I get back in his face with a closed fist.

"D, get the fuck out." Sergio pushes Arañato back and motions for me to go. I grab my purse off the floor and bounce. On the way back to my mom's house in American Falls, all I think about is that fucker threatening to do me in.

Like Sergio would ever let that happen. I know one thing's for sure: I won't do any more outcalls with him there. I mean, honestly, I could do the whole thing independently. The only upside working through Sergio is protection. If I strap up, I could do it all on my own.

My mom meets me at the front door in tears. "Where the hell have you been?" She asks frantically. I brush past her and tell her to calm down. "You disappear for two weeks—no call—no heads up! What has gotten into you?"

"Nothing!" I snap back at her. She grabs my arm and continues to grill me. "I'm fucking twenty years old! Get off my ass!" Domenica yells.

"And you live under my roof! I have a right to know where you ran off to!" She tries to make me feel like she's in control. *She's never had any control over me, ever.*

"I'm sorry, your roof?" I reply harshly, making my way into the kitchen to grab something to eat. "You never paid for shit on this house. Dad did."

"That's not the point, Domenica!"

"What do you want from me?" I ask while rummaging through the refrigerator.

"I want you to tell me the truth about where you've been. You owe me that!"

"The only thing I owe you is rent. And last time I checked, it's been paid. What kind of mother charges their daughter rent on a house that's already been paid off?" I ask while opening a pack of string cheese.

"It goes to bills; you know that." She grabs the pack of string cheese out of my hand and slams it on the kitchen counter.

"Whatever," I utter, blowing past her to my room. She follows me and slams the door behind her.

"Are you on drugs?" she asks with the gravest look on her face. I have a hard time taking her question seriously, though, given all the shit I've had to go through to earn. *Drugs make what I do bearable.*

I shake my head, knowing all she wants is for me to give her some sort of reasonable explanation as to where I've been. "Mom, I swear on my life—I'm not on drugs. The truth is I met someone and spent the last two weeks at his place."

My mother takes a moment to process and sits on the comforter next to me, seemingly calmer.

"What do you mean you met someone?"

"I'm head over heels and don't want to be apart from him. Not for one minute." I enthusiastically exaggerate the tale, but she seems to be taking the bait.

"What's his name?"

"Sergio," I reply, mixing a truth with a lie. That's the best combo for getting someone to believe what you want, especially if it's already in their head that you're a good person.

"Where did you meet?" She pries, satisfying her own desire to believe I'm not a criminal—that this is totally a valid excuse for me disappearing for two weeks. I proceed to tell her I met him through a mutual friend. She ends up believing the whole story and shrugs off her warranted suspicions. Finally, I'm able to get some sleep.

I wake up later that night and join my mom for dinner. "When am I going to meet him?" she asks, her eyes beaming at the thought of some handsome, well-off man to take care of me.

"When the time is right," I utter, taking a bite of my mashed potatoes. The guilt of lying combined with the meth comedown suddenly hits me. I begin to tear up and excuse myself from the table.

"D, what's wrong?" my mother asks, worried about my sudden change of attitude.

"Nothing, I'm just a little hormonal," I reply, wiping my eyes with a paper towel.

"You better not be pregnant," she says after taking a sip of her Ginger Ale. I share a smile with her through my tears and chuckle a bit.

"I better not be," I murmur softly, returning to the table. We have a calm rest of the evening. After dinner, we watch one of those awful Adam Sandler Netflix movies and laugh at how bad the quality of his films have gotten.

It's sort of nice coming from an extreme two weeks to a very settling environment, though I know it's only short-lived. I'll have to keep lying to her in order to get the best of both worlds. It breaks my heart in a way because I know the shit I went through as a child is somehow tied to my behavior. *The constant need for me to be in fucking control of everything.*

I wish things were different. But they're not. I am who I am, and I must own that. I truly love my mom. Each story I feed her only keeps her from further understanding the pain that I'm in.

Within the next few days, I'm summoned back into doing more outcalls with Sergio and Arañato. I apologize to the man who threatened to stick me just to keep things on an even keel.

I earn them fistfuls of cash over the course of the next year and smoke more meth than I can fathom. My mom has finally caught on, finding a dirty bag in my jeans after doing laundry. She has since banned me from coming back to the house until I get my life together.

I go until the fucking wheels fall off. It takes a while, though, almost two full years of tweaking every day to realize I'm just sucking cock to re-up my dope. My thousandaire status has since diminished, and the clientele I service has reached an all-time low.

By the time I'm twenty-two, I hit rock bottom. Blowing craigslist tweakers for shake-and-bake amphetamine isn't the most rewarding feeling a girl can aspire to have. Especially when you're willing to smoke a bowl of extended-release Adderall beads just to experience the same high.

The ice not only destroys my income but my standards as well. I finally surrender myself into the program of Narcotics Anonymous after a near-death experience with a biker who beat the fuck out of me. It's time. I mean truly, that's the last straw.

My mom attends meetings to show her support, and ironically my girl, Emm, got sober too. She found God or whatever after some spiritual hallucination during a comedown in jail.

Apparently, she reached out for help a year before I landed in the rooms and is now sponsoring people. I go through a couple shitty thirteenth-step sponsors before realizing Emma has made it a year without relapsing. She's totally capable of sponsoring me. So, I ask her, "Hey Emm, you down?"

"Course," she replies, hugging me as we make our way out of the meeting in American Falls. I've been clean for three months. Since the other sponsors didn't work out, Emma wants me to start over from step one. It's slightly upsetting because I've already done so much work on the first few steps. I begrudgingly oblige and begin again.

She's sort of a shady sponsor, though, making me feel guilty if I skip a day of calling her to check in and shit. I must remember I'm here just to kick the dope. Even if I don't believe in all the principles, it's good for me to be around folks who gave up the life of debauchery.

I've grown fond of my mom's dog, Leo. Walking him around the block three times a day helps keep me out of trouble. He's the sweetest golden retriever a girl could ask for. I'm learning to find peace amongst the simple things in life.

Mr. Carson is scheduled to get out of prison this month. From what I've heard, he's going to be moving back into the same house, right down the street from my mom and me. *Not sure how I feel about that.*

The neighbors are trying to put together a petition to have the state take his house. I doubt that will come to pass. I mean, he did his time, and I sure as hell did mine. I don't forgive him for what he did because you can't rehabilitate monsters. Though some part of me knows he is responsible for making me the person I am today.

A YEAR-AND-A-HALF CLEAN

I merge onto the freeway in my Mitsubishi convertible Spyder, desperate to get this car off the road before the cops get a make on my vehicle. *Banco Sandello—that's where I'm headed.* The only problem is Ren never told me where in Mexico this bank is located. Is it even *Google-able? Probably not.*

If I'm lucky enough to cross the border, the FBI will most likely be expecting a woman fitting my description. All because I wasn't cold-hearted enough to blast Mr. Ursaw in front of his wife. I should have, but I don't think it would have served me. It would have only made things worse. I mean, he doesn't know that I set him up, per se, just that I'm somehow connected to his fifty-million-dollar wire robbery.

The fucked up thing is I didn't get a taste of the score. I was just a pawn in Aemilian's game to acquire instantaneous wealth via a separate country.

I have maybe ten minutes until there's an APB on my back. I speed up, approaching the exit I mapped out beforehand. I take a sharp right off Palm Beach Gardens Blvd and drive slightly over the speed limit towards my destination. Shortly after Ocean Way, I bang a left into the Jalopy Jungle salvage yard and park next to a black 2007 Jetta. Thank God the lot is empty. I don't want any nosey rummagers eyeballing my shit while I'm in transition.

I exit my convertible and grab the keys off the front tire of the Jetta. The African American salvage yard worker I cut a deal with approaches. "I told you to park on the street," he says with an off-putting tone.

"I don't really have time," I reply, catching his beady-eyed scumbag stare.

"I'ma need an extra five, then."

"Take it out of the parts you sell," I reply while opening the door. He grabs ahold of the side mirror to stop me from getting in. *Big fucking mistake.* I draw my snubnosed revolver and stick it to his sternum. "Back the fuck up."

He hesitates, then slowly steps back. "You really gonna lay down lead in broad daylight?"

"Wanna find out?" I puff up, taking a step closer to him. I don't give a fuck who sees me. I'm so beyond the point of being tested it's unfathomable. He can see the red in my eyes from not sleeping. My own personal scarlet letter, indicating I've had enough.

After the "Arañato" days of hitting rock bottom and getting sober, I decided to get back in bed with a Colombian Strip club owner, Aemilian Supera. Six-months clean is all it took for me to fall back into my old ways and do things from a more calculated perspective.

Unfortunately, this piece of shit strip club owner ran a scopolamine trafficking network through the United States. Robbing trust fund babies of their net worth and leaving them without their memories was his forte. He used me and a couple other hoes to do it. After I served my use to him, Aemilian decided to leave me dead in the Everglades, which is why I'm trotting through South Florida like a resurrected harlot from hell.

"Pop the trunk," I demand, making my way around the Jetta to ensure my submachine gun quadrotor drone is still intact. He unlocks the gate and pulls the blue tarp off the drone.

"You think I'd steal your three-count felony wrap waiting to happen?" he asks in all seriousness. I slam the trunk shut with my pistol half-raised.

"Wouldn't surprise me," I say while climbing into the front seat of the Jetta. "I suggest you close up shop early and dismantle the parts… I'd hate to see another nigger in chains."

"Racist bitch," he says under his breath as I shut the door. I start the car and drive off, eager to merge onto the freeway and cut across the state of Florida. It takes several hours before I'm fatigued, but I stop to get a motel in Lucedale, Mississippi.

The scenery is far from breathtaking. Just another shitty *"we'll leave the light on for you"* Motel 6. That's their honest-to-

God catchphrase. As if they couldn't come up with something more fitting. How about, *"We house dope dealers and prostitutes and dispute all chargebacks?"* That, to me, seems more appropriate. Or at least more accurate.

I check in around 11 PM, dead bolting the door behind me. This is, for some reason, one of the tamer 6's I've stayed at—not a lot of foot traffic outside. But then again, it's before midnight.

I don't really want to be up past twelve anyway. I reward my escape from Palm Beach with a hot shower and a fresh pair of sweats. I crawl into bed and turn on the TV, but I'm fuckin wiped. I just want to sleep. I watch perhaps five minutes of The Tonight Show before shutting it off and crashing hard.

I awake the next morning with a horrible feeling in the pit of my stomach. The gut-wrenching thought of Aemilian abducting my mother has not caught up to me until now. *It's unlikely she's still alive, though I must keep searching.* He left me for dead. Why wouldn't he do the same to her?

The optimistic part of my brain wants to believe she's still breathing, but I know better than to trust optimism. Instinct is truly the only thing I have left. It's the only thing I can ever really rely on. "Fuck," I mutter, glancing at the clock on the table next to me. I crawl out of bed and throw on my baseball cap. I pack my toiletries in my tiny roller suitcase and head downstairs.

"Checking out?" the frumpy front desk woman asks with coffee induced cheer. I shake my head no, then ask her where the nearest computer is. "We have an internet café on site," she replies in an honest attempt to church-up her definition of a shithole motel computer room. I'll give her credit though; this location is one of the nicer ones.

"Where?" I ask, matching her polite expressiveness. She points down the hall and informs me that it's the last door on the left by the laundry room. I thank her before heading down the hall and make my way inside.

Just as I suspected, a clunky Windows 98 desktop with a chewed up ethernet cable jacked into it. Fuck my life, is this really what it's come down to? Three months ago, I was flying in private jets and taking scores. Now I have to use this piece of shit computer to find out where the man who ordered me dead might possibly be. On the plus side, there is a dusty hand pump Mocha machine across from the computer, thus qualifying this room as the world's most ghetto internet café.

I use the password Scotch-taped to the screen on a ripped-up piece of paper to login. It takes about four minutes to boot up. I open Internet Explorer and wait another few minutes for Google to load. If I type in *"Banco Sandello,"* there's a risk of me being tracked. So, instead, I Google *"Banking in Mexico."*

I click on the top link, which brings me to a splash page of a long list of supposedly credible banks with their address's underneath them. Hundreds of names all throughout Mexico are on this page. It takes me about thirty minutes before I see it. *Banco Sandello: Calle Ignacio Meja 302, Ciudad Juárez, 06500 Mexico.*

I grab a pen off the desk and write the address down on a

piece of printer paper. I log off and head back to the front desk with my belongings. "Miss?" I ask, interrupting the front desk woman's phone conversation. "What's the quickest way to Texas?"

"I'm sorry?" she proceeds to put the phone down and gives me her full attention. I repeat my question so she can satisfy her need to listen to what I've already asked. The woman offers to Mapquest it for me, but I don't want her searching for directions to Texas. That's another potential red flag the Feds could be looking for.

"That's all right. Just give me your best guess." I cut her off before she begins typing it in on her computer.

"Take Highway 49 into Louisiana and follow the signs from there," she says timidly while bringing the phone back to her ear. I thank her, set my room keys on the counter, and head out to my Jetta.

The seventeen-hour drive to El Paso is daunting. I manage to do it all in one shot via the help of 5-hour Energy drinks and check into a room at the Rio Grande Motel. I toss and turn for a few, but these 5-hour energies are like liquid crack. I can't sleep for shit.

I put my jeans on and walk over to the shady dive bar next door. It isn't that busy, just a couple local drunks from what I can tell.

"Jack and Coke, please," I order politely from the twenty-something bartender wearing a blue suede cowboy hat.

"ID please," he says while spitting chew into a crunched-up water bottle. I begrudgingly give him my Idaho driver's license, somewhat annoyed by the process of age verification. He surveys it for a moment before shifting his look back to me. "You's a long way from home, aintchu?"

"Yes, I am," I say while snatching my ID back. "Now, how about that drink?" I smile in a despairing attempt to manipulate this man's outlandish persona for a free cocktail. He nods, and free pours a couple of shots into a glass of ice. He shoots a baseline amount of coke into the glass with his soda gun and hands it over.

"How much do I owe you, babe?" I ask, reluctantly digging into my purse.

"On the house, muchacha. Bienvenidos El Paso," the bartender says with a heavy southern accent. I can't help but laugh at his feeble attempt to charm me with his uncanny grin. I turn away from him, finish the drink in one shot, then ask for another. He obliges my request, so I tip him with my attention and have a seat. "New out here?" he asks.

"Just visiting family," I reply wearily, not at all wanting to highlight the fact I'm headed to Juárez. I elaborate with some bullshit story about visiting my cousins. The bartender seems to believe me and asks for my name.

"D," I say over the sound of the jukebox transitioning songs. He shakes my hand and takes his cowboy hat off to wipe the sweat from his forehead

"You staying next door?" he asks. Normally, I don't tell

anyone where the fuck I'm staying, but I'm buzzed enough to let him in, so I nod yes. "I get off around two if you want me to come by," he says while putting his cowboy hat back on. I'm not surprised by his attempt to thwart me into casual sex—just seems a little quick. *It has been a while since I've been with someone my age, though.*

"If I say no, are you going to start charging me for drinks?" I ask, surveying his stance carefully with the tiny red straw pressed to my lips. He smiles back at me and shakes his head no. "Good," I reply, finishing my second round.

He offers me another, but I refuse. Instead, I write the room number I'm staying in on a napkin and tell him to come by when he's off. "It's four hundred for the hour," I whisper in his ear before leaving. I look back as I exit and catch him processing what I just told him. *Yeah, that's right, motherfucker. You want this ass, then your wallet's mine.*

At three-fifteen, I get a drunken knock on the motel door. I open wearing my pajama bottoms. Of course, it's him. It's sort of my obsession to seduce rednecks that aren't used to paying. "You really gonna charge me four hundred?" he asks while spitting into his disgusting water bottle. He's too inebriated, though. A good portion of his tobacco-stained spittle rolls down the side of the bottle onto the floor.

"You have it or not?"

"I have it," he replies, pulling crinkled twenties out of his pocket. "Had to short the register a bit, but I got it," he stutters, setting his bottle in the hallway.

"Come in, then." I grab his collar and pull him into the room. He tries to kiss me, and I immediately stop him. I don't want his disgusting chew breath anywhere near me. "No kissing, hun," I say discouragingly, shattering his hopes of some sort of girlfriend experience.

"If you don't kiss, then what do you do?" he asks, taking off his muddy cowboy boots.

"Relax," I murmur while unbuttoning his jeans. He stops me before I'm able to get his underwear off and tells me it's been a long time. I reassure him that he's in good hands and pull his cock out of his sweat-filled underwear. Before I even wrap my lips around his cock, he prematurely ejaculates onto himself. Clearly, he's not been getting any for a while—sort of strange given the fact that he's a bartender, and good-looking. I try not to laugh but can't help myself.

"Oh God." He grabs himself and lays back on the bed. I pull a towel out of the bathroom and collect my four hundred gracefully. He gets dressed, shamefully thanking me for the premature orgasm that "he" induced. I kiss him on the cheek as he leaves and encourage him to take his water bottle. I don't want that grotesque-looking thing outside my motel room. *I'm not about that trashy shit.*

"Hey, wait a sec," I stop him before he leaves. He gives me his full attention while adjusting his belt buckle. "You know a good spot around here to shoot?" He thinks for a moment before telling me about the Franklin Mountains. I write down directions from him on the tattered motel notepad.

He asks if I want him to go with me, but I tell him no. "Thanks, hun, have a good night." I deadbolt the lock and jump in the shower, considering that was the easiest four-hundred dollars I've ever made.

In the morning, I take my time scouting the mountain range. It seems a little too touristy for me. If I break out my quadrotor drone in front of a group of law-abiding Texans, they'll have my ass in jail without question. The KG-9 strapped to the base is enough to put me away for life. I need someplace more secluded.

I head back down the road in my Jetta and attempt to blast the lukewarm AC. The Texas heat in August is bad enough to make anyone wish they had a properly working vehicle. *Fuck my life. I wish I still had my beamer.* I drive into El Paso around noon and scour for a place to catch a decent meal. All I can see down the beaten path is the generic fast food chains. I'm so over McDonald's and Chick-fil-A. None of what I'm seeing looks appealing.

I end up having a pre-packaged turkey sandwich from my motel mini-fridge. I sit on the uncomfortable bed for a moment to collect my thoughts. *There's no way I can blow across the border with this sort of hardware… Nor can I test it on US soil without getting nailed by the cops.*

I finish my sandwich and head next door to the dive bar. "Excuse me?" I utter politely to the short-haired female bartender on shift.

"Yes?" She engages my stance while cleaning a foamed-up glass with her dirty towel.

"Is the guy who worked last night going to be around later?" I continue approaching the bar, taking notice of the putrid trench coat bum about to fall off his stool.

"Azul?" she asks, collecting the pile of quarters in front of the bum's empty glass of whatever the fuck he drank. I half-heartedly shrug. "He's off till Monday. You his new girlfriend?"

"Ew, no," I answer. The female bartender finishes putting the bum's quarters in the tip jar and uses a toothpick to snag something out of her back molar.

"Azul gets a lot of pussy. Hung like a goddamn armadillo snout from what I hear. You're not the first to come barging in here for seconds."

"He wasn't that big," I reply, stumped by her dismissive demeanor, and shocked by the quick-nut bartender's amount of alleged ass-traffic.

"Really? He musta done a line a coke or somethin' hun, cuz the college girls can't seem to get enough of him," she says after flicking her toothpick into the garbage can. I'm appalled by the lack of hygienic consideration for others in the vicinity. *This is a bar, not a fucking shithouse.*

"Can you at least tell me where I can find him?"

"Here, on Monday nights," the female bartender snidely retorts. I tell her I don't have that long to wait, hinting at the possibility of some serious fuckery.

"You knocked up or somethin'?" she asks, annoyed by my

persistence.

"No, but he came inside me, and I don't have enough money for the morning-after pill." My lie comes off believable. At least enough to make the bum on the barstool shoot me a drunken glance.

"For fuck's sake, how much you need?" she asks while shaking her head with a disproving look on her face.

"It's been a couple days. I should probably take a few of them, but each pill is like forty bucks," I say in a disheveled manner.

"Honey, if you take more than one, your pussy's gonna bleed like a beaver in a bear trap." The woman's tone is somewhat unnerving. She's fighting me on every level, but I have her under my charm. She doesn't stand a chance.

"So, what do you think I should do?" I ask, giving her total control.

"I'm thinkin' I give you forty bucks, you take the pill, and let it ride. Those chemicals fuck up your snatch somethin' fierce. Go easy on the nut-fuck sex, darlin'."

"I would really feel more comfortable if Azul bought it for me," I say as my eyes begin to well up with tears. The blunt bartender takes a deep breath and grabs the phone off the wall. She dials hesitantly and allows a few seconds for the call to go through.

"Azul, Barb here. Some little Latina hoochie is lookin' for you." Barb notices a small crowd of people trickle in and does a double-take towards the door. "What's your name, honey?" Barb asks while using her shoulder to grip the phone to her ear.

"D," I reply, stepping back to give the happy hour crowd some room to order drinks.

"I'm sorry, sweetie, what?" Barb asks over the noisy bar banter.

"D, as in the letter D," I reply, somewhat put off by her obvious loss of hearing. *I guess that's what happens if you work in loud settings for extended periods of time.*

"Says her name's D. She doesn't look like a gal that's gonna take no for an answer, either, so I suggest you get your pretty-boy ass down here," Barb says coldly, attempting to hurry him off the line. She takes a second and murmurs, "Uh-huh," then hangs up to serve her newfound customers.

"What did he say?" I ask, raising my voice so she can hear me better.

"He's on his way. Now, if you'll excuse me, I got a bar to tend," Barb distastefully mutters. I nod graciously before heading out the door and sit on the curb outside.

I wait for about thirty minutes and become slightly agitated. *I fucking hate waiting for people, especially tricks.* A beat-to-shit silver Ford pickup parks across the street and flashes the high beams. I stand cautiously to meet the driver. Of course, it's Azul, wearing his blue suede cowboy hat with an *oh shit* look on his face.

"So, what's the deal?" he asks a moment short of me climbing into the passenger's seat. I grab his cock through his jeans and get on top of him. My ass catches the steering wheel and makes the horn go off. "What the hell are you doing?" Azul asks as I reach for the handle to recline his seat.

"Giving you sex," I say, biting his lower lip. It doesn't take much body persuasion for him to go with the flow. He abruptly leans forward and starts to feel me up. I kiss his neck and grind on him through his jeans. "You want to fuck me, right, baby?"

"Not if you're gonna charge me again," he says with the sincerest expression on his face. I can't help but laugh while kissing him. *This poor bartender probably regrets encountering a man-eater like myself, but I'm too good to pass up.*

"I'm not going to charge you. Let's go back to the room," I whisper seductively in his ear. I don't have to convince him at all. Within ten minutes, I'm riding him without a condom in my motel room. He lasts longer than I expect. I offer him the butt to get it over with. He takes it with stride and finishes within thirty seconds.

"You're an angel," he says after letting out a breath of air.

"Awe, thanks." I stand up to grab a clean towel out of the bathroom, then realize I should probably shower.

"No, seriously, you're like heaven." Azul grabs himself contently.

"Up for a shower?" I ask, tucking a sweaty strand of hair behind my ear. He nods and follows me into the bathroom. He turns the handle to the right, making it cold as ice. "What are you doing?" I ask, quickly turning it the opposite direction.

"Never heard of a polar bear?" Azul utters with his chew-lip grin.

"Yeah, no. I don't do cold."

"Well, you ought to try it. It's great for circulation."

"So is this," I say, referring to the temperature change of the water.

"Goddamn, you're a piece of paradise," he says while grabbing the back of my head to wash my hair. I remove his hand, adjusting the showerhead so I can wash my own hair. After a few minutes of rinsing, I'm over him trying to manhandle me and jump out.

"You alright there, beauty?" he asks in his southern tone, attempting to keep his balance on the wet floor. I nod while standing and shoot him a fake smile. "I'm feelin' a little lightheaded," I say while using a towel to dry myself off.

"You don't have much stamina," he says, stepping out after me.

"Once is enough. And honestly, you didn't even last that long," I reply.

"I know, I'm sorry. I used to have more longevity before working at the shithole next door," Azul explains.

"What's your job got to do with hang time?" I ask politely, lying on the bed with my towel. Azul lays on the bed without really drying off, soaking my fucking comforter. He proceeds to go into detail about how working at the bar fucked up his sex drive because he drinks and does coke all the time.

I tell him it's all choice. "Just because you work in a bar doesn't mean you have to get fucked up." He gives me a befuddled look like something finally made sense in his life. I lay next to him in my towel and try to dumb it down a little to converse on his wavelength.

"I've thought about quitting the bar scene altogether to move back to New Mexico."

"You're from New Mexico?" I ask, pretending to be genuinely interested in his life story.

"Yeah, Santa Teresa," he says while scooting his wet arm under my back so I can lay on his chest. I go with his vibe and make him feel like my man, resting my hand on his chest.

He continues telling me it's another border town. Same shit, different city. "What brought you out here?"

"Cost of living," Azul nonchalantly mutters.

"Is it that much of a difference?"

"Well yeah. My rent out there was eight hundy for a one-bedroom. Here it's only six-fifty. Plus, you can't beat the Skull giveaway parties and authentic barbeques," Azul says as he sits up. I'm a little taken aback by his reasoning for switching states. "You know I've never done this sort of thing before with a girl like you."

"Oh, a girl like me?" I say, putting him on blast for compartmentalizing me into a category of Texan whores.

"No offense," Azul says with a backpedaling air of regret. His tone is too naive to be demeaning, though. I'm still in awe at his lack of intelligence and his baseline needs of draining his tobacco-riddled loads not being met.

"None taken," I say, sitting up next to him. Azul smiles and interlocks his fingers with mine. For a moment, I almost lose sight of manipulating. I pull my hand away and look him straight in the eyes. "Azul, I'm going to be real with you—I need some help."

I start to cry as the pain of controlling another innocent person for my own personal benefit manifests. The fucked-up thing is the tears serve me with these types of men.

"With what?" he asks in a blatant attempt to wipe my tears with his calloused farm-hand. I push him away and stand, refocusing myself. Azul rises and attempts to console me.

"I need to get across the border," I murmur softly, trying to keep it together.

Azul pauses for a moment, then asks why I would even

want to consider crossing. He continues by trying to explain how dangerous Juárez is, especially for women. "It's the murder capital of the world," Azul exclaims, desperately attempting to convince me not to go.

"They have my mom," I say, interrupting his assertion of trying to save me from myself.

"What do you mean?" Azul asks in a more serious voice. I finally give in and use the truth to convey my desperation. I tell him a relentless Colombian organization kidnapped her and that the feds are possibly looking for me. "Then you need to turn yourself in so they can help you," he says with an honest tenor of stupidity.

"I can't," I mutter, choking back the waterworks. Azul puts his jeans on in a huff and starts giving me ultimatums. He tells me if I don't turn myself in, then he will. "I didn't realize someone who paid whores could be such a fucking do-gooder," I say as he finishes tying his shoes.

"Look, this is some serious janky stuff. I can't get involved in somethin' of this nature," Azul rambles as he heads for the door.

I grab him and pull him back into my arms. He resists at first but then allows me to kiss him. I pull him towards the dresser while kissing him deep, moving his hands onto my breasts. "I can't do this," he murmurs while caressing me.

"Sorry you feel that way," I say while grabbing my scopolamine loaded syringe out from under the motel bible. I quickly jam it into his neck and slam him into the wall. "You piece of shit hick motherfucker, trying to rat me out! You will do everything I fucking say. Do you understand me?"

Azul's eyes begin to glaze over. "What are you doing?" he asks as the sedation begins to kick in.

"Taking your motherfucking free will," I say ruthlessly. Azul begins to calm from the scopolamine entering his bloodstream. Now at the mercy of any suggestion or command, I gently position him onto the bed.

I lean down to match his eye level and begin my rant of questioning to ensure the drug is already at work. Scopolamine not only takes the victim's free will—it also acts as a truth serum for those that encounter it. "How much money do you have in your bank?" I ask bluntly.

Azul tells me he's only got six hundred bucks in his account. I make him login to the Wells Fargo app on his phone to prove he's telling the truth. Or at least what he believes to be the truth. "Here's what's going to happen Azul: You're going to fill up my car, then withdraw the rest at an ATM down the street."

Azul nods in an almost coherent-like manner, seemingly lucid enough to pass as *not drugged*. "Grab the gas can out of the back of your truck and meet me downstairs. I need to finish packing," I say softly. He stands back up and nods. I give Azul his wallet before he heads out. After throwing on a miniskirt and weighing out the remaining bag of scopolamine I have left, I eventually meet him out front.

Azul waits on the bench outside the motel with the gas

can in hand and stares into the bushes. I sit next to him and lay my head on his shoulder. "How are you feeling?" I ask seductively, remembering the most important thing is to keep the dosed individual's mind calm.

"Nauseous," he says while wiping the corners of his mouth. I pull a half-filled bottle of water out of my suitcase and hand it to him. He surveys it for a moment, then takes a swig.

"Better?" I ask in a comforting tone. He shakes his head and finishes the rest. "Let's go for a drive," I say before standing. He nods in agreement and follows me to the black Jetta. We pull out of the parking lot and drive for a couple minutes down an empty road.

A few miles down, I spot an Exxon Mobile station on the left. I make a U-turn and pull into the gas station. Azul fills up my Jetta, then the gas can. He puts the gas can in my trunk and hits the Wells Fargo ATM outside. Azul returns to the Jetta with five hundred dollars in hand.

"I'm surprised Wells let you withdraw that much," I murmur as he sits in the passenger's seat. He gives me a dumbfounded look and turns his attention towards the windshield. "Tell me the easiest way to get across the border without this vehicle being searched."

"Ain't possible… Not without federales scroungin' around your floorboards." Azul wipes a bead of sweat from his forehead and rolls down the window to get some air. I shift in reverse and back out of the gas station.

"Azul, I mean this in the sweetest way possible—think

hard."

Azul turns his attention towards me as I merge onto the freeway. He presses his lips together for a moment before telling me the border security entering Juárez from El Paso is no joke. "They check cars going in and out 'cause of all the drug money flowin' back to Mexico. It ain't like it used to be."

"Then you need to think of a way that doesn't involve vehicle checks," I say while passing a dreadful: *4 miles to Juárez* highway sign.

"Santa Teresa," he murmurs through his scope-lipped daze. I give Azul my attention as he wipes his mouth, allowing him to elaborate. "It's only thirty minutes out. We can cross into San Jerónimo."

"They don't search cars?" I ask.

Azul shakes his head no and tells me that it's less enforced than the El Paso crossing. "I'd give it a fifty-fifty chance during the day, but I wouldn't chance it at night. Less traffic and a more eyes-on-you type of deal."

"I'm not chancing detainment on a fifty-fifty shot."

"Then, crossing on foot is your best option," Azul says. His comment begins to put things in perspective. *My ill-faded plan is not well thought out.* I've allowed my rage for Aemilian to cloud my judgement and put myself at risk.

Even if I make it to Banco Sandello, what the fuck am I going to do? It's a money laundering conduit. If I show up asking questions, they'll have me killed.

These thoughts don't stop me from turning my vehicle around and following Azul's directions to New Mexico. I'm past the point of rationalization. I just want to get the fuck across the border with my hardware unscathed.

THE AZUL FOOL

All or nothing, I tell myself while handing Azul my suitcase. I close my trunk and survey the port of entry parking lot for any nosey motherfuckers eyeballing our situation. Thankfully, nobody seems to give a fuck. They're too busy walking disheveled towards the Mexican border.

"Wow," Azul murmurs in awe as I grab my purse out of the backseat. *And wow is right.* The border seems more congested and locked down than what would appear to be usual for this time of night. *But how the fuck should I know? I've never been to Mexico.*

"Go ahead and cross first. I'll be a few minutes behind you," I mutter while slamming the door to my vehicle. Azul nods and cuts in front of me with my suitcase full of contraband, making his way towards the line at the port of entry's revolving doors. I begin to sweat from the humidity, taking in the notion that the feds could be waiting for my arrival. The odds don't feel great in my favor as of now.

It could just be my brain still stuck in past, trauma-induced, paranoia. I've always been able to think logically, but the risks I've taken over the previous year and the people I was associated with could put me on the FBI's fucking radar—no question.

Several people are in line. I give it a few minutes before heading towards the revolving doors. I've never actually heard of anyone using a mule to sneak shit into Mexico. But Azul is lower than a mule; he's my *hick bitch*. My scopolamine slave, rather. If they search my suitcase, it'll be his ass doing time, not mine.

I wait patiently behind a Hispanic couple and their crying baby. *How fucking annoying.* Who in their right mind crosses the border on foot with their six-month-old? For God's sake, I'm about ready to cunt punch these parents.

I spot Azul about twelve people ahead of me in line. He looks dehydrated but coherent enough to cross. It doesn't appear like they're checking anyone's bags—just a high volume of people desperate to get into Mexico.

"Que hora es?" the Hispanic man asks his wife in a low but audible enough to eavesdrop voice. She gives her answer in Spanish as I check my watch to see what the fuck time it is. *11:30 PM, not too late. Not that early, either.* I put my phone away and squint to see the revolving doors ahead of me. It appears as if Azul has made it through unscathed because I fucking lost track of him.

"Excuse me," I ask, addressing the couple politely. The woman cocks her head towards me. "Si?" She asks, wiping the sweat from her forehead.

"Why is it so busy tonight?"

"El Paso bridge is closed," the older Hispanic man says in his mucus-muddled voice.

"How come?"

"No se," the man replies while clearing his throat. He proceeds to speak to me in Spanish. I only know a little bit. Not enough to communicate effectively with my own people. The couple seems somewhat taken aback while I juggle the balance of speaking to them in English.

As I inch closer to the rusted revolving doors separating two countries, I spot Azul waiting for me on the other side with my suitcase. He seems suspicious, leaning against a Mexican food cart adjacent to three federales. The scopolamine is dehydrating the fuck out of him. One of the vendors notices his sea-legged stance and addresses him.

I cut a few people as the vendor begins to question him. "Excuse me," I hurriedly mutter, brushing past an obese woman who looks as though her ankles could burst at any moment from the cellulite. "Pinche Muchacha," she murmurs after I practically elbow her out of my way.

Azul drops the suitcase and steps away from the food cart. He begins to dry heave from the scopolamine overdose shutting his internal organs down and collapses. The federales notice Azul convulsing on the ground and rush to his aid.

I slow my roll for a moment while crossing, trying not to

draw any attention from the United States border patrol agents sitting in the port of entry booth fifteen yards to my left. Nobody seems to be watching the revolving doors going in, though, only the ones coming back to the US. Still, this whole fucking situation is shady. I apologize to the Mexican woman I cut in line and allow her to cut back in front of me.

Two United States border guards notice the commotion of Azul having a seizure on the Mexican side but don't do a goddamn thing about it. Instead, they turn to one another and laugh, almost as if it's not their problem because he's not on US soil. *Perhaps just another dope mule with a ruptured heroin balloon up his ass.* The federales proceed to give Azul CPR as I casually pass through the revolving doors.

I take a breath before approaching the food cart and calculate my move as the federales attention is still completely on Azul. I slowly reach for the suitcase on the ground behind them and push down on the handle extension. The vendor turns around right as I'm doing this and shoots me a dead-eyed stare.

"Tu sabes este hombre?" he asks as I back away crookedly. I shake my head and take off as fast as I can into the dark crowd of San Jeronimo locals.

"PARA MUCHACHA!" I hear him shout as I lift the suitcase over my shoulder and climb into the backseat of an open taxi. I can vaguely see the vendor trying to get the federales attention as they attempt to resuscitate Azul.

"A dónde vas?" the driver asks, beaming over his shoulder at my raggedy-ass entrance. I slam the door and lock eyes with him.

"Juárez, por favor. Rápido!"

"Un poco lejos," the driver mutters after acknowledging my worrisome tone. He looks to the disgruntled vendor, who now has the attention of at least one Mexican Federal Policeman.

I grab a fistful of cash from the top pocket of my suitcase and hand it to the driver. "Conducir ahora!" I impatiently shout.

"Bueno, cálmate!" he says while lead-footing the gas pedal and eye-counting the twenties on his lap. He swerves around two slow-moving taxis and cuts in front of them.

I check behind me to make sure the federales ain't tailing. I can faintly see the vendor arguing with one of them, but they're too busy with Azul's vitals failing to give a shit about some skinny-ass suitcase thief.

"Hablas Ingles?" I ask as he sets the rack of twenties on his dashboard.

"Yes," he mutters.

"Good, 'cause I don't speak full Spanish. I'll give you another three hundred when we get there."

"You in some kind of trouble?" the driver inquires, attempting to butt into my situation.

"Just drive the cab," I distastefully reply.

"Bad idea to head into the city this late."

"Did I ask for your input?" I warble harshly, taking into consideration that he's just trying to look out for me.

"No. But I assume whatever you're running from doesn't take captives… just heads."

"You have no idea if I'm running from anything," I snap as he makes a sharp left onto a well-lit motorway.

"You're right; I don't. If you are, I can't get caught up."

"Tough shit," I say while taking the snubnosed revolver out of my suitcase. The driver flinches as I jab the barrel into the back of his neck. "Keep making assumptions, and I'll blow your fuckin throat out."

"I have a family. Don't do anything stupid," the driver replies, trying to flex his third world connections.

"Oh, so you have something to lose—I don't." I say, pulling the hammer back *slowly* so he can feel the gravity of my statement. The *click* damn near makes the driver soil himself. The odor protruding from his pants is enough to know I put the fear of God into him. He begins to let off the pedal, but I dig the barrel deeper into his neck. "Test me again," I say ruthlessly.

Captain skid-mark accelerates per my request and takes me towards Juárez. We ride in silence for about twenty minutes before reaching the city.

"Here's fine," I say, motioning for him to pull over on an unlit side of the motorway. He lets off the gas pedal and swerves into the gravel.

"Please don't do this," he stammers, trying to stop himself from shaking. I reach into my suitcase, somewhat beginning to feel pity for this *pussy* Mexican cab driver and pull out another wad of cash. I set it on his lap and lower my weapon.

"I'm a broad of my word," I utter quietly, zipping up the suitcase with a calculated air of certainty. He takes a moment to count the stack and realizes it's more than what was promised. I reach for the door handle to exit as he clears his throat.

"Wait," he murmurs, trying to comprehend what just went down. I provide him a dismissive look before I'm able to open the door, begrudgingly surrendering my full attention to his glance. He clears his throat again and sighs. "This is over a thousand dollars."

"And?"

"If you think you can walk the streets with a suitcase full of money and not get robbed, then I misjudged you," he softly expresses.

"Who says this suitcase is full of more cash? Perhaps I gave you my last thousand." I smile at his attempt to try to save me, like many weak-minded men, and wave my gun to remind him I'm armed.

"That pistola holds no candle to the cartel, and their automatic weapons," he continues.

"You gonna protect me then, driver?"

"No. But I can at least take you to a formidable hotel, so you don't get mugged tonight."

"Well, aren't you chivalrous," I mutter sarcastically. He shoots me a crooked half-smirk and winces, revealing one of his silver bicuspids. *Poor fuck can't afford a halfway decent root canal.*

"This is more money than I make in a month," he says, using his left turn signal to merge back onto the motorway.

"I take it you fly straight," I reply, leaning back into my seat. He nods and speeds up, running every red light that comes our way.

"Straight?" he asks, somewhat dumbfounded.

"It means, like, not caught up," I clarify.

"The only way to stay alive in Mexico is to keep out of all the ugly things. This country is beautiful. What happens here is not," the driver says, yielding to a box truck trying to get in our lane. His statement hits all too close to home. I failed to stay out of all the ugly things in America just to satisfy my urge to earn. *Sometimes, fast money can be a surefire way to an early grave, or it can lead to a sketchy cab ride in Juárez.*

We pass some streetwalkers in front of a grimy casino downtown. One of them flashes the cab driver as he blows through another intersection. "Why aren't you stopping?" I ask.

"Not a good part of town. Mira el camión de caja," he says. I shift my attention to the box truck in the other lane. "They're scouting," he adds.

"For what?" I ask, fighting back the urge to roll my window down for a better look.

"Panocha," the cab driver stammers, yielding to the truck's right of way.

"Seems to be plenty around," I demur, gripping the handle of my pistol tightly.

"They already belong to the cartel," the driver continues, keeping both hands on the wheel.

I get the impression that anything could happen here. As if the box truck could run us off the road and help themselves to whatever they please. Then again, my brain tends to jump to severely inhospitable conclusions.

"If they already belong to the cartel, why are they scouting?" I ask, positioning the pistol closer to my side. The driver shakes his head at my remark and explains that it could be a rival cartel trying to snatch up girls to take to some other territory.

"Could just be enforcing tricks." I interrupt his thought before he can finish telling me about the area and its looming dangers.

"Tricks?"

"Clientele," I reiterate for him, damn near about to lose my patience with his English slang barrier.

"They don't really need to enforce it here. Everybody pays." The driver shoots me a crooked smile, showcasing that ugly silver bicuspid. He drives past the box truck and makes a turn onto a city block that's not crawling with whores.

A stretch of well-lit hotels is visible down the entire street. He pulls into *Hotel Lucerna* on the left side and parks adjacent to the valet stand. The cab driver takes his seatbelt off and wipes a palm-full of sweat from his forehead. "Well, this is it," he utters nervously.

"We're like one block over from the hookers," I say, not fully convinced that I should get out of the cab.

"You want safe place; I give it to you. This is the nicest hotel in town."

"And when the bellhop sees me checking in alone, how the fuck do I know he won't tip off one of those box truck drivers?"

"You don't. Bienvenidos a Ciudad Juárez."

"You're staying with me."

"Absolutely not. I have a wife and three kids that expect me home in one piece."

"You afraid of staying the night alone with a woman, or what?"

"You're no woman. You're a maneater," he mumbles in a weak attempt to raise his voice. I can't help but smile at his remark, though I take it as a compliment.

"Let's go," I order, waiting for him to open the door for me. He pauses and looks around at the people coming in and out of the hotel.

"Surely, you won't murder me in front of all these witnesses."

"Te chupare la verga. But I want three hundred back," I murmur slowly, batting my seductive eyes at the driver's mischievous look. His expression changes just by thinking about my slutty little mouth, especially because I said it in Spanish. *He fucking loves it.* I can tell he's conflicted because of his wife. Doesn't mean shit, though. Men will be men. His filthy cab driver cock probably hasn't been sucked in months.

"Seriously?" He gulps, showcasing his hideous silver bicuspid. I nod, conceal my pistol, and open the door. He follows me outside and hands his keys to the valet attendant. "What am I supposed to tell mi esposa?" the driver asks as I give him my suitcase.

"Tell her you're going out of town. Two days tops. I guarantee I'll swallow better than she does," I murmur fervently, eager to check into the hotel. The valet attendant rips a ticket from the stand and hands it to the driver. He struggles to carry the suitcase as he makes a call to his wife.

"Didn't even have to think about it?" I smirk, wrapping my arm around him as we enter the lobby. He pushes me away for a moment to chat with his wife. After an audibly disappointed reaction from her over the phone, he says something to calm her down before hanging up. "You better have the mouth of an angel."

"Guess you'll find out," I whisper in his ear as we approach the front desk. He breaks out the plastic from his wallet and pays for the room like a gentleman, eager to get his dick wet. He should have paid cash, but that's his fire to put out after the wife sees their credit card statement.

The driver grabs my hand and takes me up to the room with my suitcase. "Listo?" he asks, already unzipping his pants for me to take him in my mouth. I push the driver away and ask him to shower first. He agrees and bathes upon my request. Part of me wants to blast him through the shower curtain and take my thousand back, but I sorta need this unfaithful fuck to navigate my ass through Juárez.

After about two minutes of rinsing, he gets out of the shower and lies in bed naked. I give him my best blowjob to ensure his loyalty stays with me. He is sort of a kinky fuck, though, guiding my pinky finger into his taint. By the time he finishes in my mouth, I have three fingers up his ass with no lube and light spittle. *Didn't think that sort of shit flew down here, but whatever keeps my driver happy.*

"That was muy bueno," he says with a giant smile. I go to the sink to rinse my mouth and notice a slight amount of fecal matter on the tips of my fingers. I puke into the toilet from the unpleasant view, catching a faint whiff of his excrement. I sure as hell don't want this dirty driver's load simmering in my stomach overnight, so I puke some more.

"Everything okay?" he asks devotedly.

"Yeah," I reply softly while scrubbing my hands in the sink. "You're just a sick fuck."

"Because I enjoy prostate massage?"

"No, because you don't wipe very well." I snap, turn towards him, then wipe off with a towel. The expression on his face changes from enthralled to embarrassed.

"Are you certain?" the driver asks.

"Why would I lie?" I retort angrily as I walk back to the bed and stick my fingers in his face for him to smell.

He pushes my hand away uncomfortably and makes a face as if he caught a whiff.

"Lo siento, bonita. Occupational hazard."

"That doesn't excuse your lack of cleanliness. How would you like it if I let you put it in my ass, and I shit all over your cock?" I ask blatantly, quickly realizing he's getting turned on at the question. "Forget it."

"I apologize," he mumbles quietly. "You have the throat of a diosa. Can you do it again in the morning?"

"For the remainder of my thousand dollars back."

"Okay," he replies, totally willing to compromise his fast-earned cash for a couple seconds of pleasure—what a fucking moron. *Most men are when it comes to premeditated ejaculation.*

"Look, the reason I brought you up here is because I need a navigator tomorrow," I reply, sitting on the bed next to him.

"To where?" the driver asks while putting his skid-marked underwear back on.

"Banco Sandello," I reply. He asks me the nature of my visit to such a place, being that I'm American and everything. "You know what the owner does for a living?" I deflect.

"Every half-hearted thug in this town knows who Mr. Sandello is," the driver responds in a shrill off-putting tone. "But you can only have so much dinero in that suitcase to launder."

"I'm not washing money," I respond starkly. The driver gives me a dumbfounded look like I just tongue-fucked his sister, and he caught a whiff of my breath. "I don't work for Sandello's organization. Not anymore."

"If I'm taking you there, I need to know why," the driver presses while putting the rest of his clothes back on.

"Less is more, sir," I express clearly.

"If I'm going to help you, I need details," the cab driver bellows.

"I suggest you let my sex be your laxative to ignorance."

"You have some trouble with this man and his bank; it doesn't concern me. I can't get caught up on the losing side of some fucking war."

"Sandello's crew kidnapped my mother and left me for dead," I say, choking back tears as I stand from the bed. The driver looks at me with empathetic eyes and hesitates to speak.

"Did you owe him money?" he asks.

"Apparently, just my life. I was a loose end for his scopolamine empire. He uses it to rob the rich by luring them in with expendable whores."

The driver stands to tie his shoes in a surefire attempt to leave. "Where do you think you're going?" I ask.

"Home," the driver says. "I can't be of service to you no more."

"Oh, so what? My mouth wasn't good enough?" I ask angrily.

He pauses for a second and gives me a look. "Your mouth was exquisite… But I pity any man who must suffer the company of a woman like you," the driver says as he turns his back to me.

I can't help but well up with tears after such harsh words. *This fucker just rubs me the wrong way.*

I reach into the suitcase, draw my snubnosed revolver, and press it to the back of his head as he reaches for the door handle.

The door immediately opens before I'm able to squeeze the trigger. The handle knocks the cab driver on his ass. Several men in tactical vests bust into the room with military-grade weapons. "FBI! GET THE FUCK DOWN!"

5'2 AND BULLETPROOF

There is undoubtedly a most shameful feeling associated with being stopped from murdering an innocent person out of spite and rage. The cab driver's fate was not determined from the moment he woke up today, but by the mood I'm in right now. I mind-count the remainder of cash left in his wallet while I'm being handcuffed on the hotel floor.

"Domenica Delgado, you're under arrest for two counts of attempted murder, conspiracy, money laundering, racketeering, lewd conduct, and human trafficking in association with the scopolamine cartel." A mid-forties dominating agent yells while pressing his knee into my back. He continues reading my rights while two agents remove the taxi driver from the room.

"That about it, bad lieutenant?" I ask as he cuffs my hands behind my head. I provocatively spread my legs just to spite him. He forces them closed by brutally jabbing his M4 into my outer thigh and gets in my face.

"Listen carefully. You're in no position to add another charge to your rap sheet. And I say this without a grain of salt: if you don't cooperate, I will have your ass shipped to New York on a no-tell hold without the slightest chance of acquittal." The agent aggressively explains before removing his M-4 from my leg.

"With all due respect, I think you're full of shit. I'd have my pick of scumbag public defenders that want to make their career by taking a case of this magnitude. I'm just some girl who was forced into this by manipulative monsters that take advantage of young women. Any jury would see through prosecution the second I took oath." I rudely put things in perspective for him, unwilling to submit to his fear-based tactics.

"Even if they did, the evidence is overwhelming in your voluntary participation with the scopolamine cartel. You'd be looking at fifteen years minimum."

"You don't scare me," I say before spitting in his face. He immediately steps back in revulsion, surprised that such a disgusting gesture could come from such a gorgeous woman. A grey-haired, mid-fifties agent rushes over to bad lieutenant's side and presses the barrel of his M4 to my head.

"Spit on one of my agents again, and I'll waste you right

here, you yeast-riddled cunt." The mid-fifties agent bellows to straighten me out. Bad lieutenant wipes the spit from his face and changes his demeanor.

"Easy Ghelson, I got this," he says bluntly as if he's defending my honor.

Agent Ghelson lowers his weapon and shares a look with the mid-forties agent before he shakes his head and steps back.

"Give me a couple minutes with Miss Bala-Lolita here." He finishes locking eyes with his team as they share a look with one another. His team seems to trust the suggested procedure because they don't hesitate to clear the room.

"Like my filthy spit on your face?" I ask bluntly, trying to piss him off without regard to his intentions.

"Quite frankly, I don't take kindly to hep-c loogies being spat on me, nor do I have much respect for how tough you think you are," he harshly mutters.

"You don't know shit," I somberly reply.

"The damaged goods forced into crime routine doesn't work with me," the agent says with a shrill off-putting tone.

"Contrary to your first impression, I think you're underestimating my capability," I snidely reply.

"We've been trailing you since you left Ursaw's mansion in Palm Beach. Your little border stunt led us right to you. In my opinion, you get capability points for staying off our radar—not for leaving a trail of breadcrumbs to your arrest," the agent cockily boasts.

"You have no legal authority down here to arrest my ass," I confidently say, unaware of the bylaws they probably break just to fulfill whatever agenda tickles their fancy.

"You're an American citizen. We have every right to bring you back to the states. If I were you, I'd be high-fiving Jesus we got to you before Diego," the agent bellows. *Just what I need, a Jesus-freak FBI agent trying to flip me.* I roll my eyes at his weak attempt to play *righteous cop.*

"You want to walk away from this without incarceration or not?" he asks.

"I'll take my chances and go to trial," I coldly reply.

"You won't have to go to trial if you inform for us," he says, confident I'll bite.

"I don't know anything about the scopolamine cartel or whoever the fuck you want me to inform on," I angrily reply.

"Don't give me that shit. You backpage whores gossip with anyone who will listen," the agent says to get my blood boiling. Some sick part of me gets turned on by him rubbing my nose in his stereotypical opinion of prostitutes. But it more so pisses me the fuck off.

"I'm not a snitch," I standoffishly reply.

"It would be on a strictly need to know basis," the agent

clarifies.

"What does that even mean?" I furiously ask.

"The Mexican government rarely aids in our extradition process, despite what is perceived. Sometimes, the only way to get these snakes is to create our own mongoose. That's why we're offering you this deal," the agent says.

"You haven't offered me shit," I reply.

"I'm offering you immunity upon your cooperation. Ren Ursaw is just one of many political figures the scopolamine cartel robbed.

"That sick fuck is a politician?" I ask with a confused tone.

"Mr. Ursaw is a member of congress, as well as Jacob Maxwell. Surely you remember robbing his son in Palm Springs. Those funds were for daddy's campaign next year. You aided and abetted these thugs like it was nothing."

"I don't know what you're talking about," I hoarsely reply, unable to fathom how deep Diego's agenda is.

"These congressmen represent two-thirds of the vote allowing simplified extradition to the United States from Mexico. The scopolamine cartel's targets consist of those who expand foreign policy in South American countries, aimed at indicting the bigger fish," the agent explains.

"Why should I care?" I feebly reply.

"Because they want socialism. The current revolving door policy keeps the flow of drugs going up, and the money coming back down. With a restricted extradition treaty, these cartel bosses remain untouchable. They'll continue to thrive off the American people's addictions and use their weaknesses as capital gain," the agent explains.

"They've already done a pretty good job of that," I reply.

"We have a common goal of stopping this particular organization at all costs. The scopolamine cartel doesn't just help itself. It aids every criminal enterprise below the border by robbing these politicians. Work with us, and you'll never serve a day of prison in your life."

"You willing to put that in writing, bad lieutenant?" I mockingly ask.

"Call me bad lieutenant one more time, and I'll jam the end of my barrel up your snatch. It's Agent Moretti or sir."

"Careful, sir, I just might enjoy that shit," I flirtatiously reply.

"Let me make something clear: If you deviate from my plan whatsoever, I will leave you in the taint of Mexican hell. Got it?"

I apathetically nod, knowing my only shot at revenge is through this agent. He takes me downstairs into the lobby with my hands still cuffed behind my back. Several hotel personnel stare at us as his team escorts me outside with their intimidating, fully automatic weapons. I'm forced into the white van parked near the valet stand.

"So, dumpster dumplin' decided to cooperate after all?" Ghelson asks with his repugnant tone of old age, sitting across from me.

"Don't fuckin call me that," I snap as Moretti climbs into the driver's seat. He drives us onto the main road, barreling around slow-moving traffic like it's nothing. A part of me feels like this could somehow be a set up. But these dudes seem too American for Diego's reach.

After a thirty-minute drive, we approach the United States consulate gate on the outskirts of Juárez. This place appears to be the ultimate compound on about an acre of rural shrub. It seems untouchable to anyone even thinking of an attack, so I immediately feel safer upon its view. Four armed guards wait outside with machine guns during our arrival.

The gate finally lifts after we wait a few moments for clearance. Moretti parks the van next to a brick structure with a United States emblem plaque embroidered on the side.

He leads the way into the brick building and takes me to a set of cubicles in the back. Moretti introduces me to the Mexican American FBI director. The gluttonous existence of this individual is very unsightly with his greasy rattail hair extension. He reminds me of some of the power-addicted clients I've entertained from the Indian reservation. The nature of his physicality and job title tells me he probably has a thirst for overindulgence—be it food, women, or dominance. But then again, he could just be some fat ponytail fuck that went to Harvard and pursued the justice system.

"This is our gal?" he sternly asks Moretti with his hands on his hips.

"Director Fausto, meet Domenica Delgado."

"Nastiest snitch in the south," Fausto says to terrorize my ego.

"You kiss your wife with that mouth?" I bluntly retort.

"Watch it, Delgado," Moretti interjects. But neither Fausto nor I acknowledge his attempt to settle things down. Instead, we lock eyes and engage in further hostile body language.

"Ghelson phoned me earlier and said you disrespected Agent Moretti at the hotel," Fausto murmurs.

"And?" I ask, rolling my eyes.

"Well, if you're going to act like a twat, spitting on my agents, you'll be treated as such," Fausto explains, behaving like he's got a license to do whatever the fuck he wants down here just because it's Mexico.

"You'd probably respond the same way if a bunch of assholes with machine guns bum-rushed your hotel room, especially after just paying for it."

"The cab driver footed the bill for your disgusting oral clap transfer. His wife thanks you, by the way," Fausto begrudgingly scoffs.

"I'm sure you'd try to fuck my mouth too if we were alone in a hotel room. Shit, you seem like a backseat kind of guy, sweatin' your nuts off to get that little prick hard." I jab back with my poisonous word-vomit. *No man is exempt from treating me like dogshit.*

"THAT'S ENOUGH!" Moretti yells, displaying his bullish hunger for authority. I quickly jump back, startled by how commanding his voice is. To a certain extent, I find myself a little wet, though it could just be the humidity and handcuffs.

"*You,* missy, are the single most despicable informant I've ever had. You also may be one of the most intelligent. Reconnaissance said you survived a hit ordered by Diego's consigliere, Aemilian Supera," Fausto says, somewhat changing his demeanor.

"Did they also tell you Aemilian got me pregnant before his crew dumped me in the Everglades?" I ask. Fausto shakes his head and half smirks at my outlandish comment, waiting for me to continue. "They thought I was dead. That's the only reason I'm still alive right now."

"Shame the elements didn't finish you off," Fausto says to further get my *Mexican temper* up. I stare him down, letting him know his careless tone doesn't affect me whatsoever.

"At any rate, the scopolamine cartel might think you're gator feculence now. But come tomorrow, you're showing up on their radar," Fausto says.

"Why would I do that?" I ask.

"To kick up the manure," Fausto replies. He makes an off-colored remark about some flea market Thai food he had earlier and excuses himself to go to the bathroom.

Moretti takes the keys out of his pocket and unlocks my handcuffs. "Let's go," he says, nodding for me to follow him out the back door. I gently massage the handcuff abrasion on my left wrist and follow him outside to a shooting range.

Ghelson meets us halfway with my suitcase and sets it on the ammunition table. He unzips the main pocket and removes the quadrotor submachine gun drone, then lays it flat on the table.

"I'm surprised you were able to construct something of this nature. How'd you do it?" he asks.

"Youtube," I reply, staring him down as he attaches a 9-volt battery to the controller.

"Looks a little heavy," Ghelson mawkishly sneers as the propellers begin to flutter. I naively shrug in response to his comment and watch this dickhead step back to fly my drone.

It takes him a few attempts to keep the thing in the air, but he eventually gets the hang of it. Moretti overrides the controls and shares a look with me while exceeding the maximum elevation of thirty feet.

"I assume the trigger is to fire?" Moretti asks, using the monitor on the controller to get a bird's eye view of the drone's path.

I shrug, then cover my ears with anticipation of him leveling the dirt mound below. Instead, he takes a moment to concentrate before hardly even squeezing the trigger. The KG-9 attached to the base fires off a burst of three rounds, slicing the furthest polyethylene target in half. Ghelson high fives him as he shares another look with me to make sure I know how precise he is.

"What do you want, a fuckin purple heart?" I harshly ask, immediately tearing into his ego. Moretti passes the controller back to Ghelson and stares me down.

"I've had enough of your negative comments! You seem to think you can keep shitting on your only salvation. That isn't how this works."

"As you said earlier, agent, I'm just damaged goods."

"Do you even know what these people did to your mother? Or do you actually think she's still alive?" Moretti asks, taking another step towards me.

"If you really had eyes on Aemilian before Ursaw, you would have stopped him," I reply.

"Based on the account from her neighbor, we can make a pretty good guess she willingly left with your ex. Which means you two were double dippin' the same hombre."

"The second I found out she took off with that sick fuck, I hit the road." I say, raising my voice. Ghelson lands the drone and shifts his attention to the confrontation.

"If these people touched *my* family, I can't even tell you how personal it would get," Agent Moretti states, twisting the psychological knife into my desire for advocacy.

"Moretti—" Ghelson interrupts. But the agent puts his hand up to silence him.

"You think you can take him by yourself?" Moretti asks, rocking the boat to my breaking point.

"With all due respect, I already have. Who else do you know that's still alive after a carried-out cartel hit?" My voice cracks before bursting into tears.

Ghelson shares a look with Moretti and tells him to fuck off. Moretti goes inside, leaving me with this grey-haired agent. He gives me a couple moments to pull it together and then attempts to connect with me on some sort of cop-criminal level. He fails hard at that but allows me to regain my composure.

Two hours later, I find myself inside the US embassy barracks having dinner with these patriotic scumbags. Fausto explains that there is no time for a group hug or a PTSD mental evaluation, given my breakdown outside. They practically leave me in the dark, giving me only four hours of sleep before I'm awakened on the uncomfortable cot in my cell.

"Time to move," Moretti says, setting a sunflower dress and bulletproof vest on the end of my cot. The vest weighs down on my wrist as I attempt to pick it up with one hand.

"Are you fucking serious?" I ask.

"Put the Kevlar on under the dress," Agent Moretti says, taking a swig of his morning espresso.

"What's with the bloodstains?" I ask, nearly gagging as I survey the dress before putting it on.

"To be honest, I have no idea. One of our field teams picked it up at a dope house in Laredo," Agent Moretti says, turning his back to me while I change. He tells me to leave a layer on under the vest, so I don't chafe my cleavage. I ask if he would like to assist with said suggestion. He gets offended and steps out of the cell, telling me to stop with such provocative comments.

He leads me through the barracks towards the entrance of the building. Ghelson and Fausto intercept our departure with two other agents from my hotel raid. They're fully strapped with visible Kevlar and their M4s. Ghelson gently taps the center of my dress with a closed fist. "Good, you're all set," he murmurs, lifting my suitcase into the van.

"You're bringing my quadrotor drone?" I ask.

"It's federal property now. An extra eye in the sky never hurts," Ghelson sneers as we load up. Fausto makes a comment about the stains on my dress matching the worn-down state of my sneakers. I ignore him completely as I climb into the van with the agents.

Six people to a van feels like being packed into a can of sardines. I assume the funding for this operation is low since they're using a weapon I built against the syndicate we both hate.

"I still haven't gotten anything in writing yet about my immunity," I say to Fausto as the gates open for our departure. Two armed guards wave the van through while Moretti's impatient lead foot doesn't fail to dissipate. Fausto shares a look with Ghelson.

"Tell you what, sugar bun, you make it today without abandoning ship, and we'll deliver your letter on a laminated placard." Fausto mocks my sincerity, sharing a brief cackle with Ghelson and the other agents, minus Moretti.

"I'm not going to kiss your ass, nor am I afraid to die. You want my cooperation—document my immunity agreement on a napkin," I curtly demand.

"Bold request," one of the agents bellows. Moretti opens the glove box while submitting to traffic, and hands a note pad back to Fausto with a pen. Fausto shares another laugh with the agents, but Moretti remains still.

"Do what she asks," Moretti says, wholeheartedly having my back. Fausto acknowledges Moretti's suggestion and begins jotting something down.

"Miss Delgado, this is what my district is prepared to offer you," Fausto says, handing me the notepad. At first, his scribble appears to be the makings of a two-year old's drawing, but it's clearly a stick-figure sketch of a girl behind bars.

Ghelson looks over my shoulder and laughs. I gently set

the notebook on my lap, and stare Fausto down like the scumbag he is.

"What's the matter, Delgado, too much cock on your mind?" Fausto asks, trying to stop himself from laughing further. I change my demeanor and get the off-putting feeling that this agency is only using me as bait.

"Moretti promised me immunity."

"He doesn't call the shots down here. If I decide you do a good enough job, maybe something can be worked out. A reduced sentence, or some conjugal visitation with one of your tricks. But right now, you're mine, you little HIV-stain. We clear?" Fausto asks with a violent change of tone.

I nod in agreeance to satisfy this piece of shit's urge to be in control. Moretti drives us through the nicer part of town into a lush gated community. There's no question these houses belong to some of the bosses in control of the border.

"Just gonna roll through here, unnoticed?" I ask.

"Delgado, do yourself a favor and shut the fuck up. We have this neighborhood well scouted," Ghelson interjects.

"So do they," I respond, eyeballing a Mexican banger parked across the street in a brand-new Chevy Silverado. We pass the truck and pull into a hacienda-style gated estate.

"Just a spick doing overwatch, D. Trust me when I tell you, the cartel doesn't fuck with federal houses. Tends to shut the border down if they fuck with us," Ghelson explains while closing the garage. Fausto leads the agents and me into the house through a high-end laundry room.

We join two reconnaissance agents working from a fold-up table inside. Fausto speaks with them in Spanish and introduces me as his snitch. His disrespect doesn't sit well with me at all, as he flicks his dirty-ass rattail over his shoulder. One of the recon agents gives me a rundown on the address I'm supposed to walk to on the adjacent block.

Moretti informs me that they've done infrared surveillance from a DEA Cessna all morning, and most of these houses are clear. Apparently, four armed individuals are inside the stash house, counting an array of Colombian property deeds Diego bought using Ren Ursaw's bank wire profits.

"They just dumped fifty mil into real estate?" I ask, digging for the full spectrum of the scopolamine cartel's methodology.

"Sandello's properties are a major part of the infrastructure for money laundering. He uses proxies so the land can't be traced, putting the deeds under various people's names and LLCs," Fausto explains.

"How does that benefit him with cashflow?" I ask, confused at how this strategy could assist Diego with other people owning his shit.

"He's got more cash than God," Fausto mutters while lighting up a cigar indoors.

"All he has to do is tell one of his names to sell, and he

takes the lump sum in cash after the escrow's closed," Moretti explains.

"Anybody tries to make off with his house, or stall him; he has them trimmed. Nobody fucks with Diego Sandello except us," Ghelson says, peeking out the window.

"We need you to bring their attention outside so we can strike his stash crew with the drone," Moretti explains.

"Just keep your head down until the targets are eliminated. You don't do a goddamn thing until you count four carcasses. We'll be shortly on your six," Ghelson interjects.

"Lista?" Fausto disgustingly bellows, blowing a cloud of cigar smoke in my face.

HELL'S DOOR

I approach the house with caution, making sure the only thing following me is the FBI-controlled quadrotor drone above. The neighborhood silence is more deafening than I'd like. The unsettling Silverado is nowhere in sight. I approach the address written on the notepad in hand and take a deep breath before buzzing the gate.

"Bueno?" a familiar calloused voice murmurs on the intercom.

"Tajo," I choke, barely able to say the name of the man who left me for dead in Palm Beach. I stare directly into the intercom camera. The intercom clicks off, and the front door behind the gate opens. Three men step out with Uzis and aggressively approach the gate.

My first instinct is to run, but I immediately hurl myself onto the driveway as instructed, staring into the stucco pattern of indigo gravel-cement. The quadrotor submachine gun drone opens fire, dumping KG-9 shells all over the driveway.

I hear a quick exchange of bullets followed by several horrific screams. The echo of gunfire motivates the few vehicle-bound civilians to haul ass away from the chaos. I momentarily peak my head up as a modicum of silence soothes the air—but it's short-lived.

A flurry of automatic rounds is fired off again. A few pistol rounds fire back, and the drone crashes onto the gravel-cement, next to me. I stand and see Tajo leaned up against the gate with his pistol, losing a fair amount of blood. He limps around the corner with his gun pointed directly at me.

"Puta sapo," he stammers, grabbing his side as he sways to get a shot. I immediately spin around and bolt across the neighbor's yard. Tajo fires three rounds in my direction.

I can feel the unsteady air of bullets whizzing by as I sprint for my life. *I think I'm gonna make it.*

Another round fires off, and a crippling sharp pain in my back sends me face-first onto the gravel, near the edge of the neighbor's driveway. The agony is so dreadful I almost blackout. But the sound of Tajo's pistol dry firing point-blank to the back of my head revives me back to consciousness.

Tajo grabs a fistful of my hair and flips me over, using his free hand to squeeze my throat. He pistol-whips me with his other hand, using all his strength. Fortunately, it doesn't render me comatose; it instead pisses me off. My adrenaline kicks in, granting me the ability to rip away from his grip and bite him as hard as I can in his neck. He shrieks violently as my jaw impales his artery with murderous fury.

Tajo delivers two right hooks to my abdomen, breaking his knuckles on my bulletproof vest. Somehow, I don't let go and manage to keep my jaw clenched tight on his throat as he bleeds out. The lipemic iron in his high-cholesterol blood tastes like El Pollo Loco-flavored dryer lint.

The numbness induced by my adrenaline blocks all receptors to disgust, enforcing my defiant upper hand on his death. After about thirty seconds of vein tearing, his body becomes lifeless, and his face loses color. The federal van rolls up onto the curb through the lawn. Many neighbors watch from the street as the agents pile out of the vehicle to secure the block.

Moretti and Ghelson rip Tajo's lifeless body off me and flip him over onto the grass. Fausto and two agents secure the perimeter, turning the interior of the house upside down.

"Jesus," Ghelson says as he takes a closer look at Tajo's neck. I stand, horrified by what I've done. His neck looks as if it were torn out by a wild animal.

"He was going to kill me," I squeamishly reply, grabbing my lower back.

"You take a bullet?" Moretti asks, lifting the back of my dress to survey the damage. I nod as he yanks the slug out of the Kevlar. He holds the bullet up to show me how dense it is. "Hollow-point round. You're lucky this didn't go through."

Fausto comes outside with the agents, carrying a fistful of property deeds.

"Vamos!" Fausto yells. The banger in the Silverado speeds by the house, eyeballing the fuck out of us. Ghelson contacts the recon team on his satellite phone. He surveys the plate numbers from the truck.

"We got a Hispanic male suspect in a Chevrolet Silverado heading Westbound on Calle Misiones. Texas plates, J-145B789F," Ghelson says in a very unsettling tone.

"Eyes are on us now," Moretti says while we load up. He slams the van door and sits in the driver's seat. Fausto rides shotgun while the rest of us climb in the back.

Moretti puts his foot on the gas and swerves around the corner onto the recon block. The Silverado passes the federal hacienda a few meters ahead. We speed up as the truck drives past the intersection and loses our six.

"Put a team on that goddamn Silverado!" Moretti yells into the satellite phone, wiping a bead of sweat from his forehead. He drives down another block at fifty miles per hour.

Ghelson makes another phone call on his satellite phone. He asks for some air support, then shakes his head with a discouraged look on his face. "DEA Cessna just landed on some runway way the fuck out."

"What are you talking about?" Moretti asks.

"Propeller malfunction. Apparently, it's gonna be down till they get a mechanic on it. Military police down here won't do squat."

"Then tell our people to get back to the goddamn consulate!" Moretti blunders.

Fausto turns the radio on and lights up celebratory Cuban. James Brown's *"Papa's Got a Brand New Bag"* plays in Spanish. Fausto twists the volume knob and looks back at me with the most arrogant expression on his face.

"Uncle Sam's got a brand-new bag," Fausto smirks while he counts the property deeds like he hit the jackpot. Moretti shakes his head, clearly annoyed by the cocky nature of his boss acting half-thug. Almost as if the property deeds are now part of his personal retirement portfolio.

Fausto ashes out the window and grabs a bottle of tequila from under the seat. He takes a swig and passes it around for the agents to consume. They all drink it with a patriotic air of indulgence—even Moretti takes a shot while driving.

Ghelson gestures for me to take a sip while on his satellite phone with the recon team. He tells them to abort back to the consulate. I give him a look like he's out of his goddamn mind. He hangs up and motions for me to drink out of the bottle once more. I shoot him another dismissive look.

"Suit yourself," Ghelson says, taking a giant pull. Moretti speeds up, blowing through various crowded intersections until hitting a traffic jam in downtown Juárez. Ghelson passes the bottle back up to Fausto.

Fausto takes in his surroundings and whistles outside at some local Juárez girls in the Toyota Corolla next to us. "Que pasa un shit show traffico wey?" Fausto asks while nursing the bottle and peacocking his ugly rattail hairdo out the window.

He tucks his split ends behind his ear and offers a drink to the Juárez girls at arm's length. They most assuredly decline and roll their window up in dismay at his shoddy attempt to flirt in a traffic jam.

"You're a fucking mess," I say without fear of rebuttal. One of the younger agents tries to explain that I shouldn't offer any commentary. He's quite too good-looking to be an FBI agent if you ask me. Seems a bit full of himself, too, with his curt undertone.

"Belinsky, let the harlot-javelina spew her opinions. She ain't capable of much else." Fausto cackles while glinting back at me.

I shake my head at his buzzed state of repudiation. These feds are the epitome of the American way—authoritative assholes drowning their sorrows in booze because they need their liquid gold star to validate camaraderie to patriotism. *Classic Narcissism 101. Representing the land of the free and home of the drunken assholes.*

"Go around this Camry," Fausto demands. Moretti does his best to appease Fausto and finds himself in an even worse predicament, having to yield to offramp Juárez traffic.

"We got a correspondence problem," Ghelson says in an unsettling tone. Fausto looks back with anticipation of his mid-day buzz going to shit. "Satellite phone at the consulate's still ringing."

"Hang up and try them again." Fausto sputters, taking another swig of tequila.

"I dialed three times," Ghelson explains.

"Call Jeff's sat-cell at the gate," Fausto says, wiping the tequila from the corners of his high cholesterol, foamy lips. Ghelson grabs a geo-ping tablet from under the seat and traces the coordinates of the consulate cell phones.

"Both phones are at the consulate," Ghelson replies in a befuddled manner, dialing again. He waits a few moments without getting a response and hangs up. "Front gate isn't responding either."

"Well, they ain't out grabbing ceviche and margaritas. We may have a problem, boys. Get El Paso on the horn," Fausto says. He rolls his window up and flips off the Juárez chicks with his greasy middle finger. Fausto's knuckle hair alone is cringeworthy. The heavier traffic broad returns the gesture, and the skinny one flashes us with her tongue out.

"Nasty cunts," Fausto mumbles under his breath. Ghelson dials a much longer number and brings the satellite phone back to his ear as the whirring noise of a helicopter circles above.

"The van is in route to the United States consulate with no return answer from the gate. No, we don't have a visual. I'm requesting border support at rally-one. We have fifteen Colombian house designations in possession, all writ connected to Diego Sandello. Yes, ma'am. Thank you." Ghelson hangs up. The agents look at him for direction. The helicopter hovers directly over the van, loudly annoying most of the congested traffic goers.

"Is that a Mexican black hawk?" Ghelson sternly blunders. Moretti looks up through the windshield, flinching hard.

Automatic gunfire penetrates the roof of the van, instantly killing him and Fausto during his U-turn maneuver. "AGENTS DOWN!" Ghelson yells into the satellite phone.

An array of bullets rips through the roof, severely wounding Ghelson and killing the agent whose name I don't know. Belinsky pushes Moretti's body off the front seat to take the wheel, but our van is T-boned by a semi-truck, flipping us upside down onto the pavement.

Ghelson shrieks in agony as his collar bone shreds through his flesh upon impact, causing him to suffocate on his own hemorrhage of blood. The neck-flesh around his splayed-out collar looks like a ruptured wishbone. The sight is unimaginably agonizing.

For whatever reason, I don't pass out. Instead, I focus in. Adrenaline permeates every fiber of my being. Some biological part of my nervous system knows that to lose consciousness would mean surefire death.

The whirring sound of the helicopter grows stronger as distant sirens boom on the street. I pull a piece of glass out of my leg and reach for Ghelson's M4. Blood drips onto the stock from my forehead. Belinsky crawls towards the window and shoots me a desperate look.

"Stay the fuck down," he says, grabbing his chest in agony as more bullets rain down from the chopper. Two of them painfully hit me in the bulletproof vest. I quickly force myself under Ghelson's carcass to avoid more bullets.

The sensation is unlike anything I've ever experienced—fear, self-loathing, and gratitude for a human shield all rolled up into one hell of a mindfuck. The smell of smoldering machine-gun slugs deteriorating flesh is damn near unbearable. The echoes of screams and suffering make me wish I never dabbled down this path of iniquity.

I hear two pops, glass shatter, and the sound of this military helicopter circling back around. I push Ghelson's body off and make eye contact with Belinsky. He's been hit several times in his Kevlar and aims his empty pistol towards the broken passenger's side window.

"Still with me?" Belinsky asks, his tone shakier than before. I make eye contact with him and nod, surveying six denim-legged military boots walking towards the van twenty yards away.

"Slide me the M4!" Belinsky yells, not wasting his breath as the denim-legged military boots draw closer. Gasoline from the van leaks onto my forehead cut, burning the shit out of me. I do as he says and kick Ghelson's M4 towards him. He quickly picks it up and flicks the safety mechanism while shouldering. He fires several rounds at the boots approaching the van.

The helicopter circles back around while bodies drop in the street from Belinsky's tactical execution. One of the wounded Mexican military officials on the pavement reaches for his pistol, but Belinsky finishes him off with a three-burst kill to the abdomen.

Another Mexican military official blindly sticks his pistol inside the van and fires off a couple rounds at us. Belinsky shoots back, dropping the motherfucker instantly. Belinsky dry fires a few times and drops the M4. He grabs the tattered cluster of property deeds wedged between Fausto's corpse and seatbelt.

"COME ON!" Belinsky screams, crawling towards the back of the van with glass shards sticking out of his leg. He shoves the deeds in the cleavage of my bulletproof vest and drags me through the rear smashed window onto the street.

Belinsky picks up a machine gun from one of the bodies on the ground. He tactically snipes Mexican military officials driving up in a truck with an M134 Gatling gun mounted on the back.

Several civilians are shot in the crossfire, as the machine gun operative in the helicopter fires into the street again. Belinsky pushes me down behind the tailgate of an abandoned Prius. He squats by the back tire for cover.

Bullets thrash through the side of the Prius from above. Belinsky shoots up at the helicopter, kills the pilot, and causes the thing to crash into the overpass behind the Gatling gun truck.

Shrapnel from the helicopter disorients the other military officials near the overpass, giving us enough time to climb inside the beat-to-shit Prius. Luckily the keys are already in the ignition. Assumedly, some civilian saw what was coming and fled moments before. *Fuck, that's probably his body lying in that pool of blood in the street.*

Belinsky backs into a Honda Accord, shifts forward, and drives us across a ditch onto the opposite side of the road. He merges onto the freeway and drives away from the wreckage at eighty miles per hour. Belinsky dials a number on his sat cell while swerving around several vehicles.

"Calloway, this is Juárez Belinsky. Do you copy?" the agent desperately asks. After getting no response on two failed attempts, he frustratingly sets his phone on the center console and leadfoots the gas pedal. I scoff at his frustration, emotionally numb to the outcome. "They scrambled our sat-cell transmission."

"They can't do that," I mumble, damn well knowing that the words I use are nothing short of a self-comforting lie.

"Oh, they can't?" Belinsky angrily retorts. "Guess the hooker knows all," he mutters with a disrespectful glare.

"Don't talk to me like that," I say, furious this brand they've labeled me as discredits my every word.

"Cartels got more disposable income than Jeff fuckin' Bezos. What makes you think they don't have the technology to hit us back?"

"They don't fuck with feds," I reply.

"Those days are dead and gone. This syndicate has clearly demonstrated zero tolerance for asset repo," the agent carefully articulates.

"Then drive us the fuck back across the border!"

"We're not crossing by car," Agent Belinsky states. "They got Mexican military working for them."

Even though I'm fuming, he's correct. If not for their technological capability and military reach, we would have much less risk getting back into the United States. This is concerning on many fronts, being that this man is a highly skilled federal agent and legitimately fears his own procedural methodology to abort.

"How are we getting back then?" I protest, looking behind us to make sure we're not being tailed.

"There's a federal Cessna out in the boonies. Some shithole farm we use for counterintelligence."

"The one undergoing mechanical problems?" I ask with little assurance that this is our solution.

"Yep," he replies, also seemingly not convinced that this is our way out.

"I don't have a good feeling about that," I reply with total transparency.

"Your feelings and my training are in two completely different ballparks," the agent replies. *And he's right. I would be a skid-mark on the universe if not for his tactical expertise— nothing short of a splatter stain on the Juárez pavement.* I nod to acknowledge I'll keep my mouth shut, so he can better think through the plan.

Belinsky exits on some rural offramp, driving the rest of the way out of Juárez on the back roads. I begin to sift through the property deeds and observe the bill of sale amounts for each house.

"Holy shit," I reply, organizing them into a stack on my lap.

"Put those back in your vest," the agent sternly replies.

"He bought two beach-front mansions in Cancun," I impatiently say, ignoring his request to put them back in my cleavage.

"Thanks to you," Belinsky scornfully says. I share a look of contrition with him and do as he requests, stuffing the deeds back between my cleavage and vest.

"They promised me a piece of the cut," I hastily murmur as he swerves around an unkept pothole.

"Making harlots feel valuable is sometimes all that's needed to get things done. Aemilian and Diego are professional persuaders. You have no idea how many women went missing in Idaho and Wyoming. Some of whom were reported to have worked at the Alpine Gentlemen's club. One of our informants recalled four accounts of Aemilian sinking human remains in a geyser near Lake Palisades."

"Then why did Kasota and Jade tell me they worked for him without any problem?"

"Because he stopped recycling prostitutes after we caught onto him in ninety-seven. He beat indictment twice, Domenica. The district attorney bent to offshore funding, both occasions."

"Have they been incarcerated?" I ask, baffled that this unjust tactic could even work nowadays.

"No," the agent balks. "Budget for investigating corruption has dissipated thanks to your scopolamine cartel friends. This organization literally crippled the system. Diego throws his weight with United States lobbyists, senators, district attorneys, and supreme court judges. His arm has the most politically adept reach we've ever seen. It takes copious amounts of evidence to indict everyone on his roll, and that's only if the budget for this caseload stays uninterrupted. We've been stonewalled several times," the agent explains with a defeatist attitude.

"Holy shit," I reply as the agent finishes his spiel. He switches lanes towards the barren shrub. I look back once more, still able to see the black cloud of smoke behind us from the helicopter crash. Various news vans, ambulances, and police vehicles speed down the opposite end of the road towards the wreckage.

"Holy shit is right." Belinsky laughs at the devastation in his wake. His negligent attitude seems to serve him well amongst the chaos of his survival-based antics.

METRONIDAZOLE

We drive up on some sort of desert farm in the outskirts
of Juárez with caution. I'm assuming Diego's crew has
infiltrated this federal farm, but there are no signs
indicating such evidence. Agent Belinsky and I drive the
edge of the property. I'm shocked to see not a single soul.
The desert farm isn't even gated.

I can see a shed that looks like it's in total disarray; metal
pieces dangle off the roof, covered by a barbaric blue tarp
with stagnate water dripping off the side. This shed doesn't
even look big enough to hold a Cessna. I can't think of
anywhere else this fuckin' thing would be.

We merge off the dirt road perpendicular to a murky canal
and continue for a half-mile towards the tattered
shed, parking a few yards away.

"Stay in the car," Belinsky says, exiting with his pistol
drawn. I climb out of the Prius after him and slam the
door. He looks back at me with an earnest scowl.

"Get back in the car," he demands, obliviously unbeknownst to my rigorous persistence to ignore authority.

"Fuck that," I reply, not at all wanting to sit in the vehicle by myself. He ignores my defiance and announces his presence to the agents allegedly inside by banging on the metal siding. "Calloway, Dellstone, where you at?" he shouts, rounding the corner to the entryway.

I follow close behind him and behold the gruesome sight inside the shed. Two dead agents are impaled on the Cessna propellers, dangling a few feet off the ground, their throats brutally cut. Fresh coagulated blood is stained down their pant legs onto the dirt.

"Jesus Christ," Belinsky says under his breath, distraught by the view of corrupt Mexico at its finest. I survey the wreckage, not really surprised these guys bit the dust, knowing what I know now. Belinsky smashes his satellite phone on the metal propeller and scavenges ammunition off the impaled agents.

"What the hell are you doing?" I ask.

"Making sure these sick fucks don't track us," he replies. "Sat phone's the only way they could have found my team."

"How's border patrol gonna reach you?" I ask.

"Fuck the border patrol. They're all corrupt," he sternly replies, sharing a look of desperation with me. It suddenly becomes clear that he can no longer trust his communication on the other side of that sat cell. *His training is now telling him to go off the grid.* I begin to have faith in his judgement call, despite whether he cares what I think, and give him a subtle nod of approval.

"Grab the AK," he says while opening the door to the four-seater Cessna. I nod and head back outside, pulling the machine gun from the driver's side floor. I start to head back, but something catches my eye. After blocking the sun's glare with my hand, I can see two H3 Hummers plowing through desert weeds, about two hundred yards out.

"Hey!" I yell, carrying the machine gun back into the rat-infested shed. "Someone's coming," I say as he rummages through the cockpit, and glances back at me.

"Who?" he asks.

"Two H3s," I reply. He immediately jumps out of the Cessna and grabs the machine gun from me.

"Get in the Skyhawk," the agent protests. I do as he says and climb aboard the plane. I wait for a moment as he disappears outside. Automatic gunfire ricochets off the dilapidated shed siding. I duck down to avoid being hit and accidentally bump the Cessna ignition switch.

"Son of a bitch!" I yell as the propellers begin to run with the impaled torsos attached. They slowly scrape the dirt while spinning. One torso slides off, and the other bayonets deeper onto the propeller as the rotation speed intensifies, spraying the shed with blood.

I instinctively push forward on the yoke to try to be of some help. The Cessna abruptly taxis forward, ripping through the tarp outside. Belinsky fires at one of the Hummers and grabs onto the side of the Cessna. He opens the side door and climbs into my lap while releasing bursts of ammo into the Hummers. He manages to blow out the front tire of the yellow one, slowing it down significantly.

Unfortunately, my inefficient steering has rendered him unsuccessful to land a clear shot at the black H3, wasting the remainder of his AK-clip. The black Hummer gains on us as I swerve the Skyhawk around a dirt lump. Agent Belinsky takes over the yoke, whilst the cartel delivers several rounds into the side of the plane.

One of the rounds makes it through, grazing the back of my seat. "CLOSE THE FUCKING DOOR!" I yell at the top of my lungs. He obliges per my request and slams the Cessna door shut.

The agent forces the yoke forward, picking up as much speed as possible. I stand to reposition and maneuver myself into his lap. Belinsky pulls back on the controls, lifting the front end of the plane off the ground.

"TAKE THE FUCK OFF!" I shriek, forcing my hand over his wrist.

"DON'T TOUCH THE YOKE!" Agent Belinsky yells. We make it fifteen feet off the ground before losing altitude from my premature maneuver, plunging nose-first into the murky canal. The impact of the crash violently shatters the cockpit window, filling the cabin with giardia-laden water. The smell is gut-wrenching, and the whiplash is much more severe than the van crash.

Belinsky looks at me with *oh shit eyes,* as the stench-riddled canal water reaches waist level proportions. The Cessna's wings are completely wedged in between the canal bank, making matters incredibly stationary. *Luckily, I didn't put on my fucking seatbelt.*

Several shots rip through the body of the plane and ricochet off the metal, damn near killing us both. One of the Hummers must be right on top of us. I dive headfirst through the broken window, submerging myself underneath the plane, but the Kevlar prevents me from being able to maneuver.

I come back up for a breath of air and strip it off under my sunflower dress. Belinsky presses my vest against the side window to shield us from the bullets. Meanwhile, I unzip his vest for him. He quickly pushes his shoulders back, letting his vest slide off his body, then dunks my head with both hands. I accidentally swallow a mouthful of canal water upon submersion but continue swimming down.

I grab hold of a sharp piece of metal at the bottom of the canal to stay submerged. It cuts the shit out of my hand, but I don't let go—despite whatever infections I might be getting from this disgusting Mexican deathtrap.

The gunfire ceases momentarily. I swim back into the cockpit to get a slightly protected breath of air. Belinsky swims up with me, manifesting a clearly visible gunshot wound to the shoulder as he draws a breath. Bits of rotting dead animal parts begin to float through the cockpit.

Probably just troth slop Mexican farmers dumped from the night before. Belinsky clutches onto a rotting pig carcass floating inside the cockpit and locks eyes with me.

"Grab on," he says, looking up through the window at the Mexicans climbing out of their Hummers.

I grip the torso and instinctively dive with him as more shells rain down. We swim below the plane with the carcass and manage to get out semi-unscathed, using the torso to camouflage our heads. The current carries us away, while the cartel decimates the Skyhawk with automatic gunfire, unable to detect our departure.

The echo of shots fired grows distant as we drift away. Belinsky's breathing dissipates from his loss of consciousness. I hold his head up with one hand and keep the carcass over us with the other. The deteriorating flesh contains bacteria-masticated holes, allowing me to view the direction we're headed. I'm feeling faint as fuck, though. Either from the revolting water in my stomach or from the weight of keeping Belinsky's head above water.

I wait twenty minutes before ditching the cadaver and pop my head up for a proper breath of stench-free air. I cough unremittingly and look around to make sure the cartel hasn't trailed us. *We seem to be in the clear.*

I pull myself out with some dead branches alongside the canal bank and drag Belinsky onto the gravel. I collapse, propping my back against an old irrigation pipe. I breathe heavily for several minutes, using my fingers to stop Belinsky's shoulder from further bleeding out.

My nausea level skyrockets, and *my head feels like it's going to explode*. I grab onto the irrigation pipe and dry heave into the dirt. *No question—I caught some sort of parasite. Even just looking at the tepid canal water makes me queasy.* I kneel shakily, not wanting to endure the elements whatsoever.

"Goddamn it, Belinsky, stay with me!" I yell, jamming my fingers deeper into his gunshot wound. He comes to as the adrenaline-fueled pain wakes him up. He immediately gasps for air and jabs me in the solar plexus with a closed fist.

I lose my breath and fall to the ground, hoping he regrets this knee jerk reaction. Belinsky looks around and grips my hand, apologizing with the touch of his fingertips.

"How long was I out?" the agent asks, kneeling over me while applying pressure to his wound. I shrug at his question and hold onto my stomach. His head swivels numerous times to make sure we haven't been followed.

"We need to move," he says as I dry heave onto a dead branch. "Did you swallow some of that shit?" he queries, surveying the cut on my hand.

"Yeah," I reply. "Let's get back to the motorway," I say with a pissed off tone.

"We're not backtracking," he murmurs hoarsely, looking the opposite direction to see if there are any formidable landmarks. Unfortunately, it's just desert, dead branches, and a long stretch of canal.

"You suggesting we walk the opposite direction?" I ask with an even more pissed off tone.

"Float," Belinsky replies, holding his shoulder with one hand while looking for something we can carry into the water with us.

"You seriously want to get back in that shit?" I ask, shifting his look from the canal to my gaze.

"I don't think we have much of a choice. You're already sick. Walking is just going to dehydrate us faster," he says sternly.

"We have no idea how long this canal stretch goes," I reply, contemplating his strategy.

"So, you'd rather exert more energy by walking?" he asks, trying to put things in perspective. I shoot Belinsky an unfruitful look and shake my head, as he drags an oversized log back into the water.

"This is insane," I say, hesitantly following him back into the canal. He grabs onto the log and submerges himself into the disgusting water. I dry heave again, trying to shake off the notion that this idea could totally backfire, and submerge myself with him, holding onto the log. "We need to get to a fucking hospital."

"No shit," he mumbles as the familiar stench of rotting canal permeates.

"As soon as they find out we weren't in the Cessna, there will be eyes all over town," I state.

"They already know," he says, self-assured that the odds are entirely against us.

"So, what the hell are we going to do?" I ask, wincing from the bug-riddled canal water seeping into the cut on my hand.

"There's an abortion clinic outside of town," Belinsky utters hesitantly. I survey his look as he avoids eye contact with me.

"How would you know?" I ask.

He takes a moment before acknowledging, then looks me in the eye. "I had a girl scraped a couple weeks ago," Belinsky says.

"Don't tell me you fuck hoes," I reply. He shakes his head again, then nods.

"It was a onetime thing. I haven't seen my wife in three months." He finishes, though his statement has me questioning when the fuck he would have time. Then again, after meeting his boss, it was probably encouraged.

"Unbelievable," I say as we drift down the canal together with the log propping us up.

"I got no reason to pull wool over your eyes," Belinsky responds in a weak attempt to stay on my favorable side. He can clearly see the lack of approval in my eyes. I take a moment to get a grip on my dry heaving and use my elbow to readjust my position on the log.

We float for about an hour before hearing the rapids of the approaching Rio Grande river. The canal widens under an empty motorway, which means we're probably close to the border. Belinsky and I swim for the edge of the canal and pull ourselves out. I retch onto the dirt, barely able to pull myself up the side hill.

The thought of giving up begins to torment me as we climb. Belinsky wraps his arm around my shoulder and helps me hike to the top. He quickly flags down a semi-truck driver.

The driver nearly hits us as he pulls over to the side of the road and rolls his window down. "Que estos!?" the driver yells.

"Emergencia!" Belinsky shouts, showcasing our dire state of affairs. Belinsky explains our situation, and the driver reluctantly lets us ride with him. You can tell the stench is almost unbearable to his normal hitchhiker intake.

Belinsky gives him the address to his private abortion doctor downtown. He drives fast, not wanting anything in return except for us to get the hell out of his truck, *tout suite*. He pulls up to the gated clinic and says something disrespectful about our foul-smelling departure. Belinsky punches in the code to the gated clinic and helps me inside. The strength of his body appears almost as depleted as mine.

A few *overly pregnant* women shoot us disgusting looks as we stink up the roach-infested lobby upon our arrival. "ALFONSO!" Belinsky yells at the top of his lungs.

"Puta madre," a tan overweight Mexican man in rugged beige khakis exclaims, storming out of his private backroom. *The abortion stains are more than noticeable on his white lab coat.* "What the hell is the meaning of this?" he asks.

"Necesitamos ayuda pronto," Belinsky says with an out-of-breath tone. His face is starting to look rather pale from the untreated buckshot wound to his shoulder. The doctor opens the door to his backroom and motions for us to enter quickly. I follow Belinsky, then position myself next to a rusty medical bench in the corner. Alfonso slams the door behind us and demands some answers from Belinsky.

"Shut the fuck up and break out the gauze," Belinsky demands. The doctor tells him that he's not in the business of stitching up wounds that were meant to kill him.

Belinsky grabs him with both hands and threatens indictment if he doesn't cooperate. Alfonso takes a moment to gauge the situation, trying to come up with some conceivable reason for why we're both drenched in disgusting canal water.

"You being here puts me and my staff at risk," Alfonso answers in a weak attempt to shoe us out the door.

"I'll federally subpoena your entire shithole office if you don't treat me right fuckin' now."

"There is no extradition for abortion doctors," Alfonso interjects.

Belinsky immediately cuts him off. He threatens to make it his life's work to have the feds investigate his export business of non-FDA approved meds to the United States—if he doesn't cooperate.

"Cancel the rest of your appointments for the day, fuckhead." Belinsky finishes with a defiant tone. I honestly can't tell if he's bluffing or if he has him on an actual charge.

Alfonso blinks, noticeably fighting back the urge to leer. I don't blame him. Any doctor in his position would have to think twice, being offered such a generous ultimatum.

"Maria, cierra la oficina temprano!" he shouts through the low-budget, paper-thin door.

"Por que?" Maria yells back from the lobby.

"Por que yo dije!" Alfonso shouts back at her, rolling his eyes. "Both of you sit down," he says while rummaging through his cabinet. He grabs an empty tray and some unsavory plyers, eyeballing Belinsky's slug wound. "I'm going to tell you right now: this is not my area of expertise."

"Fine," Belinsky says as he squeezes his shoulder for a better look.

"Went in and out," Alfonso says, gritting his teeth as he shifts his look over to me. "What is your name, miss?" he asks.

"Domenica," I reply, shooting him an exhausted glance as he gauzes up Belinsky's shoulder.

"I need you to hold this," Alfonso says with a demanding tone. I don't hesitate to help. *The sooner he's done with Belinsky, the quicker he can help me.* I walk over to the agent, using the table to keep my balance, and stumble before applying pressure. "You okay?" Alfonso asks.

I give him a reassuring glance and apply pressure to the gauze as he wraps the wound. "You must have pissed off the wrong people."

"None of your concern," Belinsky fires back.

"Well, you're obviously desperate for discretion," Alfonso says.

"Why don't you focus on the task at hand and be grateful he's not indicting you—back-alley, nip-tuck piece of shit," I murmur, fighting the urge to throw up.

"Domenica…" Belinsky interjects.

"I just want to make sure whoever did this does not come here to bring me into things I don't want to be involved in," Alfonso reiterates.

"Nobody knows about this shithole, except us," Belinsky sternly says. The doctor shakes his head, and mutters something under his breath about the smell we carried in. I ignore him out of pure necessity to conserve energy.

"Keep it covered for about a week. As soon as you're able, I recommend having someone who specializes in gunshot trauma to take a better look," Alfonso explains. Belinsky nods, then shifts his attention towards my bleeding hand. Alfonso takes notice. He sits in a swivel chair for a better look.

"Okay, let's see what we can do about that hand," the doctor continues.

"Fuck the hand, doc, I need whatever you got to treat giardia."

"Pinche gringa, tienes *beaver fever.*" Alfonso grins before cackling like a maniacal backwoods fool. "All you can do about that is stay hydrated and wait for it to pass." Alfonso continues scoffing at my condition, not even attempting to brainstorm solutions.

"Can you procure me some fucking Pedialyte then?"

"Nope. Too bad you're not full-blooded Mexican." He laughs.

"What does that have to do with shit?" I angrily retort, furious that he is amused by my illness.

"Giardia tolerance is part of the gene you didn't inherit because you were born in Estados Unidos," Alfonso taunts, continuing to piss me off further.

"Laugh one more time—" I begin to threaten him, but instead of finishing my sentence, I uncontrollably vomit on his floor.

"Puta Madre!" Alfonso exclaims as the backsplash hits his khakis. He catches me before I collapse and lifts me onto the table next to Belinsky.

I'm so fucking over it; I just want to pass the fuck out. Alfonso walks back to his cabinet and rummages through a ripped box of pills. He grabs a prescription and puts his glasses on in order to read the label. He studies it for a moment, opens the bottle, then hands me two pink pills.

"Metronidazole, take it," Alfonso murmurs.

"With what?" I ask, surveying the room for something to drink it with.

"Get her some god damn bottled water, Alfonso, before I put my foot up your ass," Belinsky interjects, holding his shoulder as I put the pills in my mouth.

Alfonso digs around in his cabinet and manages to find a warm Capri Sun juice container. He hands it to me, expecting I'll just drink it with no questions asked. "They still make this shit?" I ask, placing the pink pills on my tongue.

"I don't have any bottled water, so drink it," Alfonso replies. I do as he recommends, and have a tough time taking the pills without vomiting. I finally manage to get them down, only drinking a little of the expired juice box.

"Thought you said there wasn't anything to treat this?" Belinsky asks. Alfonso shakes his head and explains he only keeps this antibiotic on reserve—for vacationers that pay top dollar after accidentally drinking Mexican tap.

"You're a real piece of shit; you know that?" Belinsky says, threatening to hit him with export charges anyway.

"You can't do that. We had a deal," Alfonso says. The feeling of thirst takes over my body. They get into a heated argument about the overall price of our visit.

I drink the rest of the juice box and throw it onto the floor, feeling a sudden influx of anger towards this scumbag doctor. I grab the scalpel from his tray and stick it to Alfonso's throat as I stand.

"Give me your fucking keys," I say with a shaky tone.

Alfonso rips the scalpel from my hand and shoves me into the wall. My head lands on the back of the end table. I drop like a sad sack of shit, unable to harbor any strength to nail him back as he lunges at me with the scalpel. Belinsky instinctively grabs the medical tray off the table and cracks it over Alfonso's head. Unfortunately, Alfonso's scalpel manages to penetrate my shoulder as he drops to the ground. "FUCK!"

I immediately pull away as Belinsky cracks him over the head once more with the tray, finishing this sick fuck off with no remorse. I rip the scalpel out of my shoulder and throw it on the ground. The nurse storms in after hearing the commotion and screams. She quickly makes a run for it, screaming down the hallway as she exits the building.

"Come on," Belinsky says, grabbing the gauze on his way out. The lobby is completely empty except for the cluster of roaches, scurrying around under the torn leatherback waiting room chairs.

"Don't ever do anything like that again," Belinsky says as I look out towards the gated entrance.

"He disrespected you," I reply, sharing another look with him. Belinsky searches the room. He finds some car keys on the receptionist's desk, then leads the way through the back door outside.

DAISY CHAINS OF MISERY

We scope out the two vehicles in the gated carport behind Alfonso's office, concluding that the key in Belinsky's hand belongs to the beat-to-shit Chevrolet Malibu. He unlocks the car as I brush past him. I climb into the passenger's seat, disheveled. I fight back the reflex to puke up my antibiotics and encourage him to hurry the fuck up.

Belinsky gets in and slams the door, shooting me a serious, concerned look as he starts the car. He douses my shoulder with gauze. "You gotta quit that hood rat standoff shit down here, Domenica. You're gonna wind up getting yourself killed," he says while wrapping my wound.

"He asked for it," I reply.

Belinsky abruptly shifts the car in reverse, then maneuvers towards the gate with a U-turn. The sensor picks up our vehicle's approach and activates the lift, allowing us to drive out onto the dingy back alley road.

Despite our putrid stench and desperate need of a shower, we don't stop for shit, until we're at least a hundred miles from Juárez. I finally manage to fall asleep while Belinsky drives us South.

I awake to the sound of the agent fidgeting around the center console.

"We need to get off this stretch," Belinsky says, surveying the desolate Mexican highway intently as he drives. The eerie feeling immediately takes root in my gut. I know he's right—I'm just not sure why. The road looks fine during sunset. Our gas gauge is now only at a quarter tank.

"How far is the nearest town?" I ask. wiping the crusty sleep goop from my eyes. I strongly notice the foul smell of our hygiene getting worse.

Belinsky gives me a look and shrugs. I open the glove box and dig through some papers, searching for a map of the area. To my own consensus, I find nothing except some rice stained burrito wrappers. *Filthy fuck probably lived from one bowel movement to the next.*

"All right, pull over and switch me so I can figure this out," I murmur, feeling much less queasy. *The antibiotics are working.*

"Negative," Belinsky says, looking from the gas gauge back to me.

"What exactly is your plan?" I ask.

"For you to shut the fuck up and let me concentrate," he says with a vile frown. We drive for another hour until the gas needle is literally past empty.

Belinsky exits the motorway and pulls into a filthy Mexican Taqueria parking lot. Five Mexican bikers hang around outside and drink Coronas. One of them does a key bump of powder and passes the bag to another biker.

"The fuck are we doing?" I ask, suspicious to Belinsky's intensions.

"You are not smarter than these people, Domenica. No matter how many of them you manage to manipulate or charm. Can't outsmart the odds of how shit is down here." The agent tries to put things in perspective for me. A few of the bikers take notice of us sitting in the parking lot and whistle from afar.

"You need to tell me exactly what the fuck we're doing here," I say, uncomfortable by the atmosphere.

"The Mexican government is too corrupt for us to find safe harbor at another US consulate in Chihuahua. We must go to Quintana Roo—Afiliados territory with untampered sat-cell transmission. I can get a coast guard to pick us up without eyes on the back of my head," Belinsky explains.

"And these bikers are going to take us there?" I ask, curious if he's trying to hash something out with them.

"Not exactly," Belinsky says, locking eyes with me.

"Then what's the deal?" I ask.

"We need to make some money to get there," Belinsky replies.

"You can't be serious," I say with an angry tone.

"They're just looking to have a good time, Domenica. The Afiliados did a lot of recon for me against SC," Belinsky says.

"SC?" I ask.

"Scopolamine cartel," Belinsky clarifies.

"In exchange for what?" I question.

"I'll ask for fifteen hundred, plus a room and shower. I'll let them know who specifically in the bureau is moving against them," Belinsky continues.

"I'm not comfortable with that," I reply.

"Tough shit," Belinsky says while getting out of the car. He approaches the bikers and talks to the head of the crew for a few minutes to get *the okay*. They all stare over at me and raise their drinks after Belinsky finishes his conversation with El Patron.

Within the hour, I find myself in a dingy rural Mexican motel shower, connected to the Taqueria. I come out of the bathroom fully naked and get whistled at by a room full of sped-up Mexican bikers. Belinsky sits in the corner, freshly showered in a plaid shirt and jeans. The bikers courteously donated this ensemble to him as part of the gangbang perk package, a few minutes prior.

He smokes a cigar while reading a Mexican newspaper, not at all interested in partaking in the gangbang—just the outcome of cashflow. He appears to be completely emotionless to the situation, which is the opposite of how I feel. The affair lasts all night. The amount of cocaine and methamphetamine these Afiliados snort is too insurmountable to keep their dicks hard.

I manage to avoid using both drugs despite how much I would like to numb this experience. I'm able to get each one of them off, after being passed around like a sex-laden petri dish.

Belinsky settles with El Patron as the sun rises, glaring uncomfortably through the blinds at people going in and out of the Taqueria next door. In a surprising turn of events, he snorts a bump of meth off the plate while I get dressed into a fresh pair of sweats. Belinsky pockets the money as we walk back to the car and starts the vehicle. He drives us down the road in total silence.

"You good?" he asks while pulling into a gas station parking lot a little bit down the road.

"Yeah, you're just a sick fuck," I reply, not really feeling like this is okay at all, but whatever it takes to get us the hell out of here.

"Not having means for transpo would have exposed us to the scopolamine cartel, stuck on the side of the road," Belinsky replies.

"You literally watched me get fucked by some trashy bangers all night and snorted bomb like it was coke. When in your career did your tarnished badge become morally justifiable?" I ask, pissed off that this even happened.

"I never said it was justifiable. I just do what needs to be done to keep myself alive. Far as I'm concerned, you should be grateful you're not decapitated in some Taqueria gutter."

"Let's just get the fuck on the road," I reply, irritated that the agent I had respect for is now tweaking in order to stay awake so he can drive.

"Fine," Belinsky says, handing me forty dollars in pesos. He motions for me to go inside the gas station to pay. *This scumbag is unbelievable.* I grab a few muffins and a bottle of water before handing the money to the attendant, then make my way back to the car.

"So, I take it this isn't your first time using?" I ask as he starts the vehicle while I sit in the passengers' seat, ready to devour this muffin.

"They cut your head off if you don't partake down here. Thinking I'm going to indict or charge 'em. The old days of agents abstaining while in the thick of it are of the past," Belinsky explains.

"Whatever you need to tell yourself to justify getting high," I reply, genuinely pissed off.

"Don't be so quick to judge. I pulled your fuckin BPA file. You fancy the same dope," he says, pulling the strings to emotionally paint me into the same corner as him.

"I've been sober from hard drugs for over a year. I'm not opening pandora's box for anybody. Not even you," I harshly reply.

"Well, who the hell else was gonna drive? Certainly not you, royal dick dynasty. We can't afford to sit stationary in Chihuahua for another day." Belinsky's tone becomes aggressive. The lack of sleep combined with methamphetamine gives him an edge that makes him very unpleasant to sit next to.

He drives out of the gas station as I eat my muffin and merges onto the motorway to continue south.

We're on the road for nearly eighteen hours before Belinsky starts to crash due to sleep deprivation. I finally switch with him during his meth come down. I begin to see road signs, advertising how many kilometers away *Mexico City* is.

I abruptly swerve off the motorway towards the stretch of Mexico City hotels and find my way to the Four Seasons valet parking line.

"Hey," I say, touching his shoulder.

"What?" he asks, wiping an amphetamine crusty from his eye as he takes in our surroundings.

"Shower and a decent day of rest," I continue.

"Can't stop." He sternly replies.

"I'm not dealing with the mood swings of your speed-addled attitude. Shower, rest, and get your head straight."

"Fair enough," he demurs, fighting back the urge to smile. The valet attendant opens the door for me, and I exit the vehicle.

"Tienes algun maletas?" the valet attendant asks. I shake my head no and brush past him. Belinsky follows. I quickly stop and lock eyes with the attendant before he parks our vehicle. "Hay un bar dentro?" I ask.

"Si, en el lobby," the attendant replies as he sits in the driver's seat and proceeds to park the vehicle.

"The fuck you need booze for?" Belinsky inquires.

"So you can sleep," I say while entering the revolving doors.

"That's the spirit," he mutters as I make my way to the bar. Belinsky splits from me for a moment to purchase the room. I order two Bloody Mary's in accordance with our much-deserved siesta and sip mine without thinking much of it.

"Gringita?" the bartender asks. I shake my head no and tell him I'm from France. Belinsky approaches the bar with his room key and nods to the bartender. *It's none of his fuckin business where we hail from.*

The bartender takes a moment to process my lie and asks how I would like to pay. I tell him to charge it to the room, but Belinsky intervenes and pays cash.

"Here," Belinsky says, swigging his drink like it's the holy grail of cocktails.

"Gracias," the bartender replies.

"I'm gonna get some rest," I say as Belinsky downs the entirety of his Bloody Mary. He motions for the bartender to pour him another one and hands me the room key. Belinsky leans into my ear and whispers, *"604."*

"K," I mutter before crossing the lobby into the elevator. I shake my head at his need to overindulge in another cocktail and push *six*. The doors close. I finish my drink on the way up and make my way to room *604* at the end of the hallway.

I have a hard time opening the door and wipe the cum smudges off the room key with my sleeve. It finally works, and I make my way inside.

The room is nicer than I expect. Then again, it is the fuckin' Four Seasons. Despite however much of a shithole the other hotels are, at least Belinsky has class in his room selection.

This horny, sped-up FBI agent chose a king suite with only one bed for a reason. *He saw me in action and wants to get laid.* I lay back on the king mattress for a few minutes before stripping down in the bathroom to shower.

Afterward, I put on the same road-trip sweats, full commando, and head back to the lobby. By the time I reach the bar stool, Belinsky is a well-composed mess—*five empty shot glasses in his wake.*

"There's my peach," he says with a serious look on his face.

"You would say some shit like that," I reply while snatching the shot-glass out of his hand and finishing it for him.

"How's the digs?" he asks.

"You booked us into a king," I say while attempting to nonchalantly hint at the fact that he wants to get laid. "What makes you think I want to share a bed with you?"

"Sleep on the floor then," he says while ordering another round.

"If you want to fuck me, be a man about it and just say so," I reply.

"Wow, you really are full of yourself," he replies with a stern, off-putting tone. "I'm a married man."

"How's that working out for you?" I ask, subtly leaning in while dismissing the bartender with my look.

"If I didn't inherit the title of *Prostitute Provisioner*, maybe it would be going better," he negatively remarks with a genuine smirk.

"Stop with the *working girl* innuendos. I never have sex with men who just snorted their brains out, so you should feel flattered that I'm willing to swallow your dirty fuckin' meth load," I murmur softly, audible enough for the bartender to overhear. Belinsky wipes a bead of detox sweat from his forehead and bites his lower lip.

"Can't say no to that," Belinsky mutters, taking my hand. I walk with him to the elevator and shoot the bartender one last look before the doors close. His jaw is practically on the floor. I don't blame him, though. *I mean, who wouldn't want me to sit on their face?*

Belinsky staggers down the hall with me like an eager nineteen-year-old on prom night. He pulls the extra room key out of his pocket with a giddy gaze and opens the door for me like I'm his sugar baby.

I casually smile at him as I enter and lay down on the bed. He deadbolts the lock behind him. I can't help but laugh at the familiarity of the situation. *I knew he was about my pussy the second he told me he knocked up some prostitute.*

"So how do you want to do this, bugaboo?" Belinsky asks bluntly while taking his shirt off.

"You could start by shutting the fuck up," I murmur seductively. He immediately tosses his shirt on the floor and takes his pants off.

Belinsky gently rests one knee on the bed and puts his cock in my face, to a certain degree teasing the fuck out of himself. I do prefer the fairer sex on most occasions, but it's all dependent on cleanliness. If it smells like meth-riddled swass, I'm usually wary of giving head.

I get on all fours and suck his balls slowly, letting saliva drip onto the bed as I slide my sweatpants off. I gently wrap my hands around his cock and move my tongue onto the tip of his perforation. Belinsky moans, reaching back to finger me while I deepthroat his cock.

He pounds my face, allowing me to cover all areas of his pleasure points. He spits on his hand and fingers my ass.

I think he's getting a little more than he bargained for. I haven't heard a man moan like this since I did anal with Aemilian last year in Alpine. Belinsky quickly rips my sweatpants from my ankles and ravages me doggy style.

We fuck for what feels like hours, but it ends almost the same as every other lay. I go unsatisfied while he drenches the fuckin sheets with an unclean load, bringing me to the brink of orgasm without ever finishing the job.

Belinsky passes out from his freshly detoxified orgasm. I grab some cash from his jeans and call down to the front desk to request some room service. They bring up a Mexican steak-salad twenty minutes later. I devour it with a plastic four-seasons hotel spork and make a mess out of the crouton crumbs in bed.

I'm able to fall asleep next to this dirty fed, catching whiffs of his meth load as a precursor lullaby. I awake several hours later to the room phone practically ringing off the hook, around 5 PM. Belinsky wakes up next to me and answers.

"Yeah?" he mutters with an exhausted yawn.

"I'll be down in a few," he says as he sits up in bed and hangs up the phone.

"Who was that?" I ask with a cautious tenor.

"Chill out—I forgot to settle up at the bar. Last few drinks were apparently put on the room. We don't have a credit card on file, so…"

"How much do you owe?" I ask.

"Fifty," Belinsky replies.

"Let's just dash and hit the road," I say with a standoffish tone.

"Fuck that. We'll leave in the morning. Let's grab some dinner," he mutters while putting on his ugly plaid shirt. I put on my sweats and head downstairs with him.

We make our way back to the bar and settle. I purloin a fifty out of Belinsky's jeans while he flirts with the female bartender on duty. I hit the gift shop to buy a fresh pair of panties and sneakers. Belinsky follows me in after his mid-evening flit. He buys a hat and some underwear. I pay the cashier and grab a bite with Belinsky at the hotel restaurant.

"How much we got left?" I ask while shoveling a forkful of mashed potatoes into my mouth.

"Five hundo," he says with a stoic look of certainty.

"That's enough to make it to Quintana Roo?"

"Gonna have to be. I don't know anyone outside Chihuahua. Unless I pimp you out on a corner."

"Yeah, that's not happening," I reply.

"No shit, D. Lighten up," he says while fighting his 7 PM yawn. I shrug and finish my meal, not sure whether to take him seriously.

"You're literally impossible to read," I reply, half-flirting, but also trying to gauge his intentions.

"Supposed to be," he says softly while shelling out cash to pay for the meal.

"Why is that?" I ask, surveying his expression closely.

"Part of the job," he replies.

"Mine too, I guess," I beckon hesitantly.

"What job? You're unemployed, damaged goods." He scoffs, fighting back the urge to laugh more than he needs to in order to make his point.

"Excuse me?" I ask.

"Only thing you got going for you is avoiding serious prison time," Belinsky rudely explains.

"I could say the exact same thing for you!" I start to raise my voice but catch myself before it gets too loud.

"No, you can't," he replies.

"Yes, I can. You're dirty as fuck!" I boast, feeling heated that he thinks he can be just as corrupt without any consequences.

"Congress passed a *no-holds-barred* exemption for any branch of Interpol facets in Mexico, including FBI. Third-world country, third-world policies," the agent explains.

"Which validates you acting like a total piece of shit down here?" I ask.

"It exemplifies me from facing charges if a period-stain like you decides to open her mouth about our operation in Court. Jury is subject to overlook such behaviors because they're based out of necessity, rather than criminality."

"A thug with a badge is all that is," I murmur loudly.

"That's your perspective, not the eyes of the Supreme Court's."

"What the fuck ever," I reply, leaving the table and heading back to the room.

The following morning, breakfast downstairs is shoddy. The same bartender from yesterday practically buys my breakfast, then propositions me to ditch Belinsky and stay with him in Mexico City. I end up giving him the finger while finishing my last bite of huevos rancheros. I meet

Belinsky outside by the valet stand. I can feel his eyes on my ass the entire stride to my departure, through the revolving doors of the hotel.

Belinsky takes a drag of his cigarette and surveys my freshly showered look.

"Morning," he says with a calloused smile.

"Fuck off," I reply, blowing past him into the car.

THE SICK ARE NOT WICKED

We drive nonstop through Veracruz, Tabasco, Campeche, and Yucatan, only to arrive in Quintana Roo within twenty-two hours.

Belinsky pulls into the US Consular Agency parking lot on the beach. He takes a piss in the Mexican sand out front and lets out a sigh of relief. One of the Mexican American armed guards approaches him and tells him that he can't do that in public.

Belinsky gives out his badge number while putting his dick back in his pants and surveys the guard's intensity before opening his mouth. "I need to speak with the Consular communications director immediately," he says in a demanding tone.

The guard motions for him to come inside. It takes two hours before anything substantial surfaces. The communications director gives me an off-putting vibe. The phone calls he makes to the FBI office and US coast guard seem off. He leaves to take a bathroom break. I ask Belinsky nervously, "This guy is US government, right?"

"Domenica, we're good here."

"I just—I'm not getting a good feeling about this whole thing."

"I haven't had a good feeling since I graduated from the academy. Feelings are overrated. Learn to deal," Belinsky bluntly states.

"What if he's on the cartel's payroll," I ask, concerned that this could be a legit possibility.

"Very unlikely. We've given no indication of our whereabouts, technologically speaking. SC is geographically connected, but they're not magicians. They wouldn't hit us this close to Navy and Coast Guard."

"Bullshit. They attacked us on the fucking border," I reply, losing faith in the desired outcome.

"Un-bunch those paranoid panties and sit tight," Belinsky replies.

"Or what?" I ask.

"Or I'm gonna cuff you while we wait," Belinsky mutters.

As soon as he says this, I dart outside. My trust has completely gone away with men. I've been fucked over too many times not to allow myself to overthink. Belinsky comes after me and grabs my arm.

"Domenica!" he yells, startling a few tourists upon his approach.

"LET GO OF ME!" I yell, going into full meltdown mode. Belinsky grips on tighter as I clench my fists. I instinctively swing on him, but his training is way too advanced for my reach. He grabs my fist like a feather and puts me in a chokehold.

"FUCKER!" I yell, furious that he's forcing me to do what he wants.

"Calm down," Belinsky says in an eager tone, not giving a shit how many onlookers take notice.

"I'LL SCREAM RAPE!" I yell, sure that this plan will work. Unfortunately, he starts laughing and squeezes me into a more intimate chokehold.

"Be my guest," Belinsky says, unable to wipe the smirk off his face while leaning in to kiss me. I lean back to get away from him, but trip over his shoe. I fall on my ass into the sand. He laughs while reaching his hand out to help me up. I push his hand away and stand on my own.

"You think that's funny, motherfucker?" I ask, stopping myself from laying hands on him.

"Yeah, I do." Belinsky fires back.

"I don't trust this plan," I say, unable to fathom all the emotions I'm confronted with. *He's so god damn handsome; it's hard to be pissed.*

"You don't trust anything. Railing copious amounts of speed over the years probably fried a synapse or two," Belinsky says after clearing his throat.

"I've been off meth a lot longer than you, thank you," I utter in a pissed off tone.

"Under eighteen months?" he asks with an animated smirk.

"So?"

"Post-acute withdrawals can last up to two years," he explains, totally blowing off the fact that he touched glass two days prior and sweat it all out on the sheets.

"How often have you been bumping it?" I ask, redirecting the focus back on him.

"Just when the occasion calls."

"Often?" I pry, trying to gauge his addictive tendencies.

"I got high before I joined the bureau, D. This shit ain't anything new."

"Why the fuck would they hire an addict?" I ask, blown away that this is even a possibility.

"Are you shittin' me? Half of our cybercrime division in Langley tested dirty during their initial UA's for marijuana. Some of the best hackers in law enforcement used to be stoners. Going from their mother's basement to the academy."

"What's your point?" I ask, not really giving a shit about his proletarian spiel.

"I had five years clean before I signed up. Beauty of Narcotics Anonymous is that it's anonymous."

"I'm blown away they didn't dig deeper with you," I reply, surprised by his innate justification.

"Perhaps they did and still hired me anyway. Only thing that makes a good cop exceptional is someone who knows the game and thinks like a con. Cookie-cutter bullshit doesn't work against higher-ups. We have to fight just as dirty as them to stay alive down here," he replies.

I nod, acknowledging the fact that this agent just happens to abide by his own rules. Some part of me questions his loyalty to the law, but it does sort of make sense that he must fight dirty.

"You think I'm gonna let you get done in?" Belinsky asks, tucking a sand-riddled strand of hair behind my ear. He tries to get intimate with me, using his calloused hand. I shrug with a sincerely *baffled* look on my face.

"If I wanted you dead, I would have let them kill you in Juárez," he says with a lighthearted air of reassurance.

"You said so yourself: Everyone in government has the ability to be corrupt."

"The bounty on your head isn't as high as you think. Besides, if I wanted a piece, I wouldn't be taking shots at the guys with cash," he says through his pursed lips while kissing me. I finally accept that Belinsky isn't going to lead me into the mouth of hell and go back inside with him. The consular communications director greets us inside. He wipes a bead of sweat from his forehead.

"Have a good shit?" Belinsky asks with his smug-to-the-point tone.

"Coast guard is meeting you in thirty minutes here." The communications director points to a dock on the map. He hands Belinsky a temporary US Government ID card and satellite phone. Belinsky picks up the atlas and surveys the rally point after pocketing the phone and ID. He nods to the communications director and thanks him before leading the way back outside.

"What's going to happen?" I ask as we get back in the car. Belinsky shifts the car in gear and drives us out of the sand-laden parking lot.

"I don't know. I need to call Carter at Langley and see what's what," Belinsky murmurs.

"I mean with me," I curtly reply.

"You'll probably be in wit-sec solitary for a year awaiting trial. I'll vouch that you've been cooperative with the bureau as our confidential informant, but you'll still be looking at five years minimum for conspiracy."

"Jesus fuck—I can't do five years," I say with an honest, fearful tone.

"Well, you don't actually know anything the agency can use regarding Diego and Aemilian's whereabouts. You were purely our *flush em out* gal," Belinsky explains while putting on a pair of sunglasses from the center console.

"That's so fucked," I reply.

"I don't make the rules, D," Belinsky replies, rubbing my arm. I think hard for a minute as we approach the dock next to a Carnival cruise liner and come up with a quick proposal.

"I saw SC's stash house in Bogotá."

"Yeah, and I'm guessing you don't have an address for me, do you?"

"What is your deal?" I ask, furious he's gone from lovey-dovey bad cop to non-corrupt Mormon lieutenant in a matter of seconds.

"I'm just giving it to you straight, D. You're serving solitary time—no questions as to that. You'll be in wit-sec after you get out."

"You used me," I reply, making sure he knows how displeased I am.

"Don't twist my intentions. I didn't use you. This is my job," Belinsky clarifies while he parks near the dock. Several tourists take pictures nearby, coming off the cruise ship.

"Just let me go, and I'll get on my knees for you again. Otherwise, I'll find a public defender hell-bent on crucifying you personally. Hair follicle tests, sexual misconduct allegations, old NA sponsors on the stand type of shit. By the time my public defender is done burning you, it'll be your ass in prison for obstruction instead of mine."

"Wow, if you didn't suck cock for a living, you would have the makings of a legitimate dime store attorney. Several decrees protect my decision-making down here. So, pound salt, cunt," Belinsky says. But before he can finish the word *cunt,* he's met with my fist to his nose, harder than I've ever hit anyone in my life. I hear the bone break as blood spills out onto his shirt and horrifically dribbles down his chin.

Amid his shellshock, I bolt out of the car and make a run for it into the luxurious Temptation Resort lobby. Belinsky calls my name out behind me. My freedom depends on his meth-withdrawal kicking his ass, stamina-wise.

I race across the banquet hall and exit the opposite end of the resort, barreling my way through some palm trees near a cab stand. I jump into a monochromatic blue taxi, and say "Vamanos," in a suspiciously alarming voice. The driver doesn't respond, and Belinsky gains on the vehicle.

He opens the door and pulls me out by my hair. I

aggressively kick outward, but he pins me in his familiar chokehold, flashing his tarnished Government ID to onlookers nearby. *Fuck this piece of shit.*

"You busted my nose," Belinsky says while forcing me onto the ground, pressing his boot onto my back. He uses his sat cell to call the coast guard and gives them our coordinates. Within twenty minutes, I'm handcuffed by three armed United States military officials and forced onto a small coast guard boat.

"Good lookin' CI," one of the coast guards says to Belinsky.

"I've seen better," an older coast guard replies. They all share a laugh, except for Belinsky. Belinsky glares at me with a tampon string hanging out of his nose. The boat operator fires up the motor and takes us out to sea without much hesitation. The sound of the engine is too loud for me to hear anything they're talking about. The sights of Quintana Roo harbor are breathtaking. Dolphins swim near the bay, behind the Carnival cruise liner, and capture my focus on our way out.

We sail through the ocean for thirty minutes, past the commercial fishing boats, and make our way towards a large Navy ship on the outskirts. The older coast guard picks up his binoculars and grabs the others' attention. Belinsky snatches the binoculars and has a look. "Son of a bitch," he says, grabbing a pistol from the dry storage container.

"Tell the Beaumont to dispatch backup!" one of the coast guards yells over the roar of the engine. I can see the outline of two black boats coming towards us. The unsettling feeling in the pit of my stomach begins to take over as the operator turns the boat around and heads back to shore.

"Son of a bitch," Belinsky says, raising his sat cell to his ear. "You were right," he continues, referencing my paranoia at the communications director being dirty. Belinsky struggles to get any sort of signal, as do the coast guards.

"Doesn't make any sense. We're not in a dead zone," one of the coast guards' says, unable to get a frequency on his radio.

"Sat scramblers," Belinsky says as he takes another look through his binoculars. The two black boats have already cleared double the distance we have and are only about a hundred yards on our six. One of the coast guards takes a bullet to his torso and nearly falls overboard. The older coast guard grabs ahold of him and tries to stop the bleeding while keeping him from falling over the side of the ship.

"STAY DOWN!" Belinsky yells as I peek my head over the motor. He pushes me to the floor and covers my head as buckshot splits the back panel of the boat. Two of the coast guards shoot back with their M4s. The boat operator fires a flare up into the sky. *Like that's gonna do us any good.*

I hear the exchange of gunfire for several seconds, then the thunderous bang of a military jet dropping altitude. I peak my head up for a moment and see an array of gunshots decimate the cartel boats, killing everyone aboard both crafts. Both vessels sink almost instantaneously. I look up and see a Navy-bound F-16 buzz the skyline, circling our boat to provide additional cover.

Belinsky yanks me up by my handcuffs. He forces me to sit on top of the storage container so he can tend to the wounded coast guard. He applies pressure to the man's chest, but the wound is so severe that the coast guard dies upon resuscitation. The static noise over the radio is interrupted by a muddled transmission, "Coast guard, this is USS Beaumont, Air Marshall Douglas McKinney, copy," the voice echoes, sounding all too familiar. *Could this be the same Douglas McKinney that had me arrested for going AWOL before I decided to get back into stripping?*

Belinsky grabs the radio and raises it to his jaw. "McKinney, this is FBI Agent Garret Belinsky. I have one coast guard casualty on board, two unscathed, my CI and myself, over," Belinsky says as the coast guard operative steers the boat around, towards the navy vessel. The F-16 buzzes over us again in an intimidating sweep, providing a disturbing *don't fuck with this boat* allure to any potential threats wanting to continue the attack.

The USS Beaumont opens its bow doors for us to board the well dock inside. The same McKinney who put my ass in military jail, not more than fourteen months ago, stares me down as we drift inside. Two Navy officials pull us onto the well dock.

Agent Belinsky yanks me off the boat by the back of my handcuffs and offers his rugged hand out to McKinney. McKinney shakes it and introduces himself, commanding two of his Navy officers to tend to the dead coast guard on board.

"*You're* the reason one of my crew members lost his life today?" McKinney asks in his pissed-off tone.

"You two know each other?" Belinsky asks, confused by the sergeant's transparent familiarity.

"I see you've been demoted to Navy," I mutter, cutting through the bullshit of his outlandish persona.

"Navy is the second cousin of spring break, Delgado. I get to travel the world. Doesn't look like much has changed with you, though. Still gussied up in tarnished handcuffs," McKinney replies.

"This going to be an issue?" Belinsky asks as one of the military officials drags the dead coast guard onto the dock.

"I'll leave it up to the bureau to make the D.O.A. call to Eric Radford's wife and two kids, jackass," McKinney mutters while surveying his comrade's body.

"Easy," Belinsky says in a standoffish tone. "You don't want to be collecting retirement benefits out of a tin can on the side of the freeway, do you?"

"Go to hell," McKinney retorts as he takes a step towards Belinsky to intimidate him.

"Fuck your mother's cunt," Belinsky declares, letting his speed-withdrawn temper get the best of him as he challenges McKinney's stance. The coast guards intervene and come between both egomaniacs in order to settle the tension.

"At ease, gentlemen," A coast guard says, staring both Belinsky and McKinney down with an egregious gape.

"I did my due diligence with this hooker's manipulative antics after she tried to determine her rank at Hill. I want minimal interaction while she's on board. Keep her on a tight leash." McKinney states.

"Dishonorable discharge, wasn't it?" Belinsky asks. I shake my head at his attempt to suddenly share a moment of law-abiding peace with McKinney, just because they both have government clearance.

"Now, what would a cartel counterintelligence fed be doing with a skid mark like Delgado?" McKinney inquires after clearing his throat.

"Fuck you," I reply with slight hesitation. McKinney doesn't even flinch. Instead, he seems to get off on my rebuttal.

"Not much I can tell you, except an H-16 transporter is on the way from Cape Canaveral," Belinsky articulates.

"I was told it would arrive at thirteen hundred tomorrow. Transcripts stated subject is a *high flight* risk. Little did I know it was miss AWOL," McKinney says as he locks eyes with me.

"I'm sorry, what bad blood with my CI do you have besides abandonment, McKinney? Did you two have a moment of indecency on the base?" Belinsky inquires with a snakey-ass, double-edged allure. McKinney's face goes beat red. *Not because we ever fucked, but probably because he's obviously fantasized about it.*

"If chiggers could fly." McKinney sneers.

"Let's disperse with the pleasantries. Quite frankly, I haven't had a decent shower in weeks. How about you show us where we're staying so I can freshen up?" Belinsky suggests, ignoring McKinney's subtle jabs on my behalf. McKinney showcases his biggest vile smirk to date and nods to one of the coast guards.

"Give these two the royal suite, Jevon," McKinney says. Jevon, the African American coast guard, offers him an overenthusiastic salute. I catch McKinney staring at my butt on our way through the ship-hall corridor, and quiver in disgust.

We take the stairs two flights up and reach a grip of overflowing dishracks outside the connecting door. This must be the messiest ship of soldiers I've ever encountered, leaving their dirty dishes in the stairwell and shit.

Jevon holds the door open for us as we enter the cabin hall. He lets his foot off the entry and cuts back in front, leading us down the empty corridor. Jevon opens a spray-painted metal door and leads the way into the dingiest boiler room I've ever seen. Two adjacent cots are positioned next to the hot water heater with questionably moist sheets.

"What the fuck is this?" I ask, offended that anyone could suggest such a condition for us to stay in.

"Be grateful for what you got. You's a long way from home, honky bitch," Jevon mockingly murmurs.

"Kid, you want a future with your government or not?" Belinsky asks.

"You think I'm stupid?" Jevon asks with a cocky smirk.

"Get us a decent room, and I'll make sure your resume gets to the top of the pile at the bureau after your tour here."

"I don't want to be an FBI Agent," Jevon replies.

"You would rather clean mess hall soldiers' shit instead of doing real service?" Belinsky judges. Jevon pauses for a moment. A serious look comes across his face.

"Look man. I ain't no suit-wearin', James Comey-ass motherfucker. I'm a coast guard," Jevon mutters with a false sense of pride.

"Listen to me, dickhead. Despite what your boss thinks about us getting your comrade killed, it was the bad guys who pulled the trigger. Now, please get us a standard room."

"Have a nice evenin'," Jevon says, leaving the door open as he heads back down the hall.

"Guess that dirty badge of yours is really more of a lead balloon," I murmur as he takes the tampon out of his nose.

GRADES OF SHADE

"What say you to a dribble of Mexico's finest whiskey?" Belinsky asks with a half-cocked grin. He takes a swig from his recently boosted ship-hall flask upon entering the boiler room and offers me a swig. I despairingly shake my head and turn away from him on my cot. Being handcuffed to the hot water heater makes it hard to reposition.

"I'm not getting drunk with you in this disgusting boiler room," I reply.

"Oh, but you really should reconsider. Time flies when you're staying loose," Belinsky says as he sits on the adjacent cot. I shake my head, furious that this guy has acted like the opposite of a cop from the very start.

"I don't let external forces dictate my ability to stay coherent," I reply.

"I would retort by suggesting you make a mountain out

of this shitty boiler-room molehill."

"Go to bed," I reply.

"You gonna punch my lights out if I don't?" Belinsky cockily sneers. I ignore his childish prodding remarks until he finally drinks himself to sleep.

I awake the next morning to the sound of F-16s buzzing the naval ship. Breakfast in the mess hall upstairs is five *stars* despite their lack of staying on top of dishes. It's as if the sergeants running this vessel believe they're on permanent vacation.

Belinsky and I receive a thorough check-up by the onboard female physician. His buckshot wound has become slightly infected, and the physician pays special attention to his hangover. "How much have you been drinking?" the navy physician asks.

"Not much. Last few days, give or take," Belinsky replies as the physician finishes applying fresh gauze to his wound.

"I'll just be curt with you—lay off the cocktails while your body is trying to heal. It interferes with your immune system and leaves you prone to infection." Belinsky shoots me a *keep your fuckin mouth shut* glare as the doctor finishes looking him over. "Other than that, you're fine."

"Great, thanks," Belinsky says while putting his shirt back on.

"How long ago were you two exposed to this Juárez canal water?"

"Three days ago," I reply.

"And *you* had symptoms of giardia, but not *you*?" she asks. I share a look with Belinsky and nod.

"Antibiotics subdued the vomiting for the most part," I reply.

"Do you remember how much you took?" she asks while feeling my forehead.

"One pill," I respond.

"Well, you don't have any of the side effects I see with giardia patients. You're also very well hydrated, so good on you," the physician states. "Any other exposure to the elements?"

"No, but we have been given the shittiest room on deck. Anything you can do to alleviate those conditions?" Belinsky asks, looking the doctor directly in the eye with his *hair of the dog* stare.

"All due respect, detoxing in nicer quarters isn't going to make any difference to the physical nature of your condition."

"What the fuck does that mean?" Belinsky asks.

"I can smell the whiskey on your breath. I recommend some sleep before your transport arrives."

"Doctors orders?" Belinsky interrupts.

"Bet your ass," the physician says. I can't help but share a look with her and smile. "The upper deck is a pleasant place to sweat it out. F-16s are doing drills this morning. That should do wonders for your inevitable headache."

"Last thing I need is the sound of a jet engine in my ear," Belinsky replies.

"Fresh air will do you good," she says without fear of rebuttal.

"You a friend of Bob's?" I ask the physician flat out. She pulls up her sleeve and shows off her service, unity, and recovery tattoo on her wrist.

"Oh, for Christ's sake. Two broken birds on the same haul," Belinsky speaks before handcuffing me. I thank the doctor as he drags me back into the hallway. We head back to the boiler room in a bedraggled fashion.

I watch him drink another quarter bottle of whiskey that he must have pawned from the mess hall. He passes out for a *solid* few hours. We get a loud knock on the door around 1:15 PM. It takes a few moments for Belinsky to come to. He finally opens the door for Jevon.

"Transport is on the helipad," Jevon says. Belinsky uncuffs me from the hot water heater and rips me from the cot. He re-cuffs my hands behind my back. We follow Jevon to the top floor and are greeted by several navy soldiers, the transport pilot, and a well-dressed transport agent.

"I'm afraid we have some news, Belinsky," the transport agent says in a calloused manner. Belinsky waits for him to continue, but he doesn't. Perhaps he's just trying to hide the whiskey on his breath. He refrains from breaking the silence. McKinney approaches with the freshly printed transcripts in hand. He gives them to the transport agent and shares a look with Jevon.

"Your confidential informant doesn't have clearance to come back," the transport agent says.

"What the hell are you talking about?" Belinsky asks.

"Carter doesn't want to waste American tax dollars indicting her on a federal *no-tell* hold. She doesn't know anything of substance we can use to continue this case."

"You're stonewalling her?" Belinsky asks.

"We're in international waters. Domenica Delgado is no longer considered a person of interest at this time," the transport agent explains.

"They'll kill her if you just dump her back in Mexico," Belinsky responds.

"That's not really a US government concern. The Sandello case is an unvarnished waste of resources. If she attempts re-entry, she'll be denied. Her United States citizenship has been denaturalized."

"The girl was born in American Falls, dickhead. She's got birthright."

"Her refusal to testify before congress, and a list of heinous racketeering crimes, makes her a burden on the system, unfit for correctional convalescence. She's a waste of US tax dollars."

"She will testify," Belinsky says, trying to defend me.

"Carter himself signed her deportation papers. We've got bigger fish to fry. McKinney will see to it she's dropped off on the coast. Let's go," the transport agent beckons before turning around.

"This is bullshit," Belinsky says, attempting to give me a reassuring glance. I don't even try to argue against these consequences. I know this is the corruption that goes hand in hand with SC infiltrating the system. *Sandello and Supera want me dead bad enough to the point they probably had to bribe someone high up to get this thing signed.*

"Put your personal feelings aside, Garret. You're being reassigned to Langley," the transport agent says with a filthy air of patriotism. Belinsky shoots me a sincere apologetic look and boards the H-16 with the transport agent.

"Drop her off on the next rotation, Jevon. I want this hooker out of my sight," McKinney says as the H-16 helicopter takes off. Belinsky locks eyes with me from the window and takes a swig from his American flag flask, almost as if he has something up his sleeve. Perhaps that's just my optimistic thinking trying to autocorrect the doomful outcome of my reality.

I shake my head—furious that SC has this deep of reach.

There's no way in hell the Afiliados can have any sort of leverage against SC with their exasperated crystal meth use. Even if Quintana Roo is part of their territory. Jevon and another coast guard escort me down to the well dock. They force me onto the coast guard boat like ungracious cargo. Jevon climbs in and fires up the motor.

"Anything to say for yourself?" Jevon asks.

"You're very naive to jump back on this boat in international waters," I reply as the other coast guard unties the dock rope while climbing on board.

"What do you think this is for?" Jevon asks, showcasing his refined M4 as the other coast guard steers us out to sea. I smile at Jevon's ignorance. In turn, it makes perfect sense why McKinney uses him to do high-risk, frontline activities.

"You have the keys for my handcuffs?" I ask as he loads a couple of intimidating rounds with one hand and pulsates his index finger on the safety with the other.

"Just my bitch cutters," Jevon responds.

"Wanna do the honors?" I ask, gauging his intelligence. He shakes his head, ignores my question, and locks in on the shore.

After twenty minutes of uncomfortable waves aggressively smashing against the bow, we approach the docked cruise liner. I scan the shore for anyone suspicious enough to do me in. Surprisingly, I see not a grade of shade in sight.

The chatter of American cruise line aficionados reaches earshot as we drift into the semi-crowded port. I keep my eyes peeled for peril, but still see nobody menacing enough to raise an eyebrow. *That's sort of the point with how they operate, though.*

Jevon forces me out of the boat onto the boardwalk.

"I'd say you fell out of the manure truck smelling like a turnip," Jevon says as he snips my cuffs on the boardwalk. A few passerby's take notice of the handcuffs falling onto the boardwalk from my wrists.

"Ignorance really must be bliss," I murmur. The sound of metal hitting the wooden dock should be the sound of freedom. But I'm not free at all. I'm a slave to death's infinite attempt to entomb me in some drab laden, cantina shithole. *Despite how beautiful Quintana Roo is, there is nothing pretty about what goes on here.*

"You're not facing any charges, and you landed in one of the most progressive places in Mexico. Do something positive with it," Jevon says with an uplifting tenor.

"Anything else, black Tony Robins?" I reply.

Jevon shakes his head as he climbs back into the boat. The other coast guard steers the boat around. I watch for a moment as they sail off, grateful I don't have to deal with that entitled coast guard prick anymore. I make a B-line towards the nearest hotel and do my best to blend into the crowd with scrupulous caution.

I walk fast, damn well knowing that the more crowded of an area I'm in, the safer my chances are at slipping into the abyss of Mexico's independent escort trade. As I pass by a boardwalk coconut stand, I'm met with the uncomfortable familiar grip on my shoulder from behind.

"I hear you've been looking for me, princessa," Aemilian finishes his sentence as I quickly spin around to make sure what I'm hearing isn't some post-traumatic stress hallucination.

Sure enough, the murdering scumbag is right before me in the flesh, wearing beige khakis and a hemmed Armani blazer. Two well-dressed Mexicans stand near him, seemingly unarmed. But I know they're packing heat under their fucking summer suit jackets.

"Where is she?" I ask, astonished he has the balls to face me directly.

"You'll be with her soon. Vamos muchacha, ahora," Aemilian says in a demanding way.

"Fuck you."

"I missed that dirty little mouth of yours, princessa," Aemilian says as he grabs my arm.

"You want me dead—be a man and do it right here, YOU CONNIVING PIECE OF SHIT!" I scream at the top of my lungs. Several tourists take notice as one of the men grabs my arm. I punch him as hard as I can in the throat. He grabs his neck in pain as Aemilian's other consigliere flings me over his shoulder.

Several bullets ricochet off the coconut stand from an unseen shooter, killing the innocent vendor inside. The man who has me draped over his shoulder takes two bullets to the chest and collapses onto the boardwalk. His corpse somewhat shields my impact as I land stomach-first on the dock. Blood drains out through the boardwalk fissures and drips into the ocean. I quickly climb to my feet to get a grip on what the hell is happening.

Several tourists shriek as more gunfire echoes from what appears to be two Mexicans in front of a black SUV parked on the beach. Aemilian and his remaining throat-punched consigliere draw their concealed machine pistols and fire back at the black SUV, killing the men in front of the vehicle.

"Do you want to survive?" Aemilian asks in a very thunderous tone. Some part of me thinks perhaps he didn't order Tajo to murder Kasota and me that night in Palm Beach. *Perhaps there are other elements I don't know about.* I feel in my gut if I don't give myself to him in this specific moment, I'll wind up dead from the crossfire. Though the fight or flight part of my brain realizes that this is exactly what he wants me to think and that I shouldn't trust him at all.

My train of sensible thought is interrupted by more rounds fired off from atop the cruise liner. As Aemilian's remaining throat-punched consigliere is gunned down, I instantly realize Ameilian is in some internal war with Diego Sandello. I grab his hand and allow him to lead me behind the coconut stand.

"FUCK!" I yell, losing all hope to a much-deserved outcome of tranquility.

"KEEP YOUR HEAD DOWN!" he screams as numerous bullets rip through the air from two different directions. Aemilian shoots back at the cruise ship assailant with his machine pistol, killing several tourists in the crossfire.

The exchange of gunshots continues as we run through the row of vendor stands towards the edge of the dock. Aemilian loads another magazine into his machine pistol, looks towards the edge of the boardwalk, and fires back at the cruise liner assailant. He grabs my hand and yanks me off the dock. The eight-foot drop doesn't make the sand as soft as one would think upon landing nose first on a washed-up log.

Aemilian yanks me up before the painful severity of my broken nose manifests. He guns down an innocent tourist riding an ATV and climbs on the back in a very animalistic fashion. He yanks me up onto the back. My nose bleeds all over his blazer as he drives up the shore towards a coastal road. Gunshots ricochet off the sand behind us as a motorcyclist steers off the road.

The motorcyclist attempts to fire off rounds at a twenty-yard distance but is interrupted by Aemilian's preemptive ability to shoot first. The motorcyclist takes a bullet to the shoulder and crashes into a coral boulder with an umbrella sticking out of the crevasse. The motorcycle flips over and lands on top of a few tourists sprawled out on a picnic blanket, and the rider is killed instantly upon impact.

The carnage of Aemilian's survival-based tactics not only rekindles the fire but somehow restores the notion that perhaps Diego ordered everyone from the Alpine crew to be killed after the indictment charges, including Aemilian.

Could this perhaps just be wishful thinking? It's the only plausible explanation as to why bullets are raining down on my former flame. These men could also perhaps be an arm of the Afiliados trying to kill him, or it's some internal war amongst the scopolamine cartel.

Aemilian accelerates the ATV and merges onto the main road. He cuts in front of a silver Porsche at a traffic light and jumps off. He aggressively showcases his machine pistol as a warning to the portly Mexican guy in the driver's seat.

The portly Mexican guy in the Porsche tries to swerve around him but is gunned down upon fleeing. Aemilian opens the door and drags his body out like an animal carcass. He fires several rounds into the portly guy's abdomen. He waves for me to jump in after spitting on the body like a piece of sewer trash. Several cars and onlookers flee quickly after seeing his careless rage in broad daylight.

I acknowledge he has every opportunity to kill me but doesn't. The instinctive part of my mind tells me not to get in the Porsche with him under any circumstances. I ignore my gut feeling and climb in willingly. His gratuitous violence is despicable, though some part of me wants to hear his side.

"Where is she, Aemilian?" I ask urgently as he blows through the red light and sets the machine pistol on the center console.

"Hang on," Aemilian says, driving fast through a series of red lights. I catch a glimpse of two motorcyclists trailing behind us in the rearview mirror. Aemilian takes notice and speeds through a bad neighborhood to lose them. He cuts through an alley and goes the opposite way into oncoming traffic. Aemilian swerves around again, driving fast under a bridge the correct way. He looks over his shoulder, damn well making sure he lost the tail. To my eyes, he seemingly has. I snatch the machine pistol off the center console and raise it to his cheek.

"Where the fuck is she?" I demand. But Aemilian doesn't even flinch. This crazy fuck's *gangster ego* is too far stretched to be afraid. Instead, he laughs in my face.

"YOU WERE THE LAST PERSON WITH HER BEFORE SHE TOOK OFF!" I yell while trying to stop my nose from bleeding with my free hand.

Aemilian laughs with a horrendous maniacal grin. I've never seen him this emotionally whacked out. I press the hot barrel of the Uzi into his cheekbone. He lets out a razor-sharp shriek and pulls away. I'm quickly greeted with a giant smack to the face as he snatches the gun from me. He throws it out the window like a disposable camera, then swerves into a shitty barrio.

SCOPOLAMINE

"Show her the room," Aemilian mutters as we enter a hole in the wall apartment in Cancún. I look back at the Porsche parked outside and hold a section of crinkled postal stamps to my nose in order to stop the bleeding. I'm greeted by the cringe-worthy, gap-toothed grin of the balding Alpine Gentlemen's club manager, Dustin Sparks.

"Hey D, long time no see." Dustin reaches out for a pit-stained hug in his tropical toucan blazer.

"Don't fucking touch me," I reply, backing away.

"Fair enough," Dustin responds, nodding for me to follow him into one of the spare bedrooms. "Got a surprise for you in here," he mutters while opening the door. I hesitantly peak in the room. The Alpine gentlemen's club house-mom, Jade, stitches a tissue box with my actual mother, Orquid Delgado. They're both sitting on a blowup mattress with no sheets. My mother jolts up as if she's seen a ghost, then locks eyes with me.

"Domenica?" she mumbles. I immediately cover my

mouth in shock before hugging her. Dustin and Jade clear the room as we tearfully embrace, her tissue box still in hand.

"I thought you were dead," I murmur, wiping my eyes.

"No, Domenica, I've been here," she replies.

"How?" I ask, baffled by her mellow attitude.

"Aemilian is a good man. He's been taking care of us," my mom says in an autopilot tone.

"No the fuck he's not," I reply, quickly stomping out her insistent naive belief that there can be no evil in this world.

"He told me you would react this way," she says.

"Are you sleeping with him?" I ask in an immediate attempt to cut through the bullshit.

"How could you even ask me that?" She turns away and scoffs.

"If you're not having sex with him, then he obviously fucked with your head," I say, beginning to lose my patience.

"I left willingly."

"Why the fuck would you leave the country willingly with a stranger?" I ask in a defiant tone.

"I started to believe him after I couldn't get ahold of you.

After all, Aemilian is *family*," she replies with a Manson-like lack of empathy.

"Mom?" I ask, beginning to realize the lights are on, but she's far from home.

"I always trust my gut. You know that," she demurs with a scopolamine-like slur.

"When did he put you under?" I ask, surveying her glance intensely.

"Aemilian kept reassuring me you were still alive. He refused to finish Diego's orders," she completes her vacant blanket statement, tightening her grip on her tissue box. I back away from her and nod.

I storm out of the room and stand directly in front of Aemilian with a menacing frontage. Jade shoots me an effervescent stare as I shift my look to her.

"We're not such bad people after all. Are we, D?" Jade defiantly queries.

"Shut your fuckin' mouth," I retort.

"You gonna shut it for me if I don't?" Jade sneers.

Aemilian stands, then backhands her in the face. He tells her to shut the fuck up and forces her into the back room so she can sew another tissue box. Jade slams the door on her way in, giving Aemilian and me some discretion. Aemilian opens a bottle of vino with his stolen Porsche key and takes a swig like the sloppy-natured gangster he is.

"All I ever wanted was to protect you." Aemilian lies as he holds out the bottle for me to drink. I decline and ask Dustin to step out onto the porch for a smoke.

He nods without hesitation and respectfully pulls out a pack of camel menthol lights. Dustin steps onto the dim porch. I sit on the sofa across from Aemilian and survey him closely.

Two bikers pass by the porch in non-menacing attire. Dustin nods to them as if they're neighbors. He takes a drag of his cigarette with unsuspecting certainty that everything is okay. *They could easily pass as tenants due to their casual sweats—fairly intelligent of the Afiliados bangers.*

"I was pregnant when Tajo dumped my body in the glades, Aemilian. I have every right to believe you were behind all of that."

"Diego ordered it, Domenica. I made him believe I had every intention of carrying it out to protect you," Aemilian responds.

"I don't buy that for a second," I tell him.

"Why would I go through the trouble of keeping your mother alive if I didn't care for you?" he asks, then pauses before swigging another pull of wine from the bottle.

"So, you would have your ace-in-the-hole story to save face in case I survived. I think you believe I could be of service in helping you murder your boss. Once Diego's dead, you gain control of SC, and I've served my purpose.

Right?"

"Always such a paranoid mija." Aemilian chuckles and draws a silencer from under the couch cushion. He points it directly at my head. "If I wanted you dead, what's to stop me from pulling the trigger right now?" he asks with a half-serious look on his face.

"Because you have it in your head that I can move past you dosing my mother with scopolamine. I think you believe I would see your manipulation as some sort of gesture of goodwill because you didn't murder her. Or maybe you think I would choose the *ignorance is bliss route* for my own financial gain. Unfortunately, neither of which have come to fruition."

"You're too loca for your own good," Aemilian mutters as his face turns red from the wine and lies.

"I was your best asset, Aemilian. It's too bad you weren't smart enough to realize that and cherish me for what I had to offer. Our kid would have been fucking beautiful," I say quietly as he pulls back the pistol hammer with his thumb.

"If you can't find it in your soul to view my actions as sympathetic, then this is it," Aemilian reiterates.

Two of the citizen-dressed Afiliados open the unlocked door and arm-bar Aemilian into the couch before he has any clue to what's going on. Aemilian's drunken stunted reaction hinders him from fighting back.

He fires off a round during the struggle. The bullet blows a hole out of the back of the couch cushion next to me, sending cum-stained couch fabric particles into the air. They manage to take his gun and force him into submission with a serrated knife to his throat.

One of the bikers holds him down as the other begins to decapitate him alive with the serrated blade. The horrendous yell is unlike anything I've ever heard.

Aemilian's voice softens as the biker saws through his vocal cords and cuts all the way through the back of his neck. He yanks Aemilian's head off his body like it's a slice of factory, farm-grade meat, then gives me a look like he did me a favor.

Dustin scrambles inside from the porch to get a grip on what the fuck just happened. He drops his cigarette as the biker holds up Aemilian's head, then staggers at the power shift in the room. The serrated knife-wielding biker drops Aemilian's head on the couch and sticks the flesh-riddled blade to Dustin's throat. He grabs ahold of Dustin so he cannot escape.

"No neccesita este mierda, si?" the biker asks with a thick Mexican accent, looking to me for guidance as the other biker locks the door behind him.

"Did you know what your boss was planning?" I ask as Jade storms out of the room in a confused frenzy. The biker without the knife points Aemilian's gun at her head. She stops dead in her tracks, horrified by the amount of blood on the couch.

"NO!" Dustin pleads while a bead of sweat drips from his forehead onto the knife. The biker holding Aemilian's gun pulls the trigger before Jade can beg for her life, pumping the bitch full of lead.

Her body hits the ground hard. She struggles to get a few blood curdled breaths of air while dying on the floor. The biker stands over her body and fires a few more rounds into her face to make sure the job is done, then fastens the patio curtains closed.

"I'm going to ask you once more. Don't think so hard this time," I continue, shifting my gaze back to Dustin.

"I – I – Didn't know what he wa-was gonna do! I swear," Dustin stutters.

"He was going to use me, like he used you, and then dispose of all of us after Diego's murder had been successfully carried out. He wanted ultimate control of SC," I reply, reaching for the bottle of wine on the table. I take a swig and give him a menacing glance. "No more suck jobs, right, D?" I ask, mocking the first time he ever thwarted me into sucking his cock at the Alpine gentlemen's club.

"I SWEAR ON MY LIFE I'LL NEVER ASK FOR THAT AGAIN! DON'T KILL ME, D! PLEASE!" Dustin begs as he wets himself. Tears stream down his cheeks like the pussy I always knew he was.

"Where is Diego's scope house?" I ask.

"I – I – DON'T KNOW – EXACTLY," Dustin burbles as the biker mounds the blade deeper into his throat, drawing some deserved blood.

"It's a simple question," I continue, taking a step over Jade's body towards him.

"He's got dozens of scope houses, D." Dustin whimpers.

"Don't give me that shit. You damn well know the one I need access to," I persist, full well understanding he's just buying himself time.

"I can take you to the main one in Colombia as insurance you don't waste me right fuckin' here," Dustin counters.

"Don't listen to this fool, D," the biker with the gun interrupts. I ignore him and share a look with Dustin.

"How long has she been dosed?" I ask.

"Two weeks, off and on," Dustin sobs.

"Can you find me the drug that counteracts it?" I ask.

"Nothing counteracts it. Just time and rest," Dustin mutters.

"Then get me a glass from the kitchen," I say earnestly.

"Wh-wh-y?" he cowardly stutters.

"Because I'd like to offer you reconciliation while we discuss what needs to be done. Unless, of course, you prefer to drink from the bottle like your former employer here."

"I don't drink anymore," Dustin says.

"Then grab two glasses for them," I murmur. Dustin furrows his brow and looks from one biker to the other. Neither of them will let him move an inch.

"I don't trust this gap-toothed piss-stain meandering around for one second," the biker holding the knife to Dustin's throat states in his Spanish-muddled accent.

"I take it you two got the call from Belinsky?" I ask the biker holding the gun.

"We got the message from El Patron to trail you from the pier. Belinsky has intel that Aemilian's connection in Langley delivered a hefty severance fee to a retired FBI agent—*now congressman*—in order to fulfill your deportation papers. Aemilian Supera is as dirty as it gets."

"What do I owe you for stepping in?" I ask.

"Disposal of this mierda rata. You cannot just leave our enemies mouth intact." The biker holding Aemilian's gun explains.

"Dustin is not a rat. He is loyal to whomever wields the blowjob or pocketbook," I say without fear of rebuttal.

"He's loyal to the idea of escaping the blade. This coward is liable to say anything under the threat of death," the biker wielding the knife says.

"BULLSHIT!" Dustin retorts. The biker aggressively slams him against the wall.

"I need him alive," I say.

"Not a shot in hell," the knife-wielding biker replies.

"Let me the fuck go!" Dustin whimpers.

"He's got the scope house coordinates. Hold the fuck off!" I bellow as tensions rise.

"Belinsky can geotag the location from Aemilian's satellite phone. This piss stain is of no use," the biker reiterates.

"THEN AT LEAST ALLOW ME TO DO IT HUMAINLY!" I yell, furious that they're not listening. The bikers exchange a cautionary glance before deciding that this is a reasonable idea.

"Fine, Chiquita," the biker with the gun says. He places the silencer in the palm of my hand, then stands next to me as I aim at Dustin, almost like he's astounded I came to my senses.

"D, I'M BEGGING YOU! DON'T DO THIS!" Dustin squeals. The biker holding the knife attempts to hold Dustin still as he squirms for his life.

I quickly shoot the biker standing next to me point-blank in the head, then fire two more rounds into the knife-wielding biker. *Unbeknownst to them, I have military training, and I fucking hate when men don't give me time to think.*

Blood pours out onto the ground as their bodies hit the hardwood. Dustin's leg quivers as he sobs, clearly shocked by my methodology. I set the silencer on the couch next to Aemilian's severed head and give Dustin a sincere, apologetic look.

"Look at me." I grab Dustin's chin and force him to acknowledge what I just did for him.

"I have faith in your ability to get me to Colombia. Now compose yourself and get cleaned up. You're going to take me there."

Dustin wipes tears from his eyes and apathetically nods, then does as I ask. After he gets cleaned up in the shower, he helps hydrate my mother with an IV drip back in the room. She lays down on the blowup mattress and takes a much-merited nap.

Dustin shows me where the remaining stash of scopolamine and cash are being held. He finally pulls himself together after realizing I'm not going to do him in. He shares a look of contrition with me as I unscrew the air conditioner vent near the inflatable mattress.

"Can I ask you a question?" Dustin beckons. I nod while removing the screws and set them on the wine-stained carpet. "Why did you spare me if some fed you know has access to the coordinates?" he asks as I remove the cover and pull out the powdered bag of scopolamine on top of the money.

I shrug, not really giving his question much thought. I weigh the bag of scope out on the scale near the inflatable mattress, then seal off the bag with my crusty hair tie before pocketing it. "Why is that relevant?"

"I just want to make sure you're not playing me to get there," Dustin hesitantly demurs.

"You should be kissing my feet, you sick fuck."

"You're right—I'm sorry," Dustin responds.

"You prefer to be dead?"

"I just don't know how much more of this I can take. Going against Diego Sandello is like committing suicide— only hanging yourself would be a lot easier."

"Just shut the fuck up and load the bag," I reply, pulling the ten-thousand-dollar wrapped bands of cash out of the air conditioning vent. We begin stacking in separate piles and combine the outcome—a *hundred and fifty large.*

"Jesus Christ. I couldn't even do a midday focaccia run without Aemilian commenting on the receipt and change back." Dustin comments.

"He was a frugal fuck," I reply. Dustin shakes his head, furious his former employer was holding out on spending when he had it.

I grab the inflatable mattress bag from the floor and load the money into it. I shove a ten-thousand-dollar banded stack into Dustin's pocket. He spins around, paranoid I'm trying to harm him, then realizes I'm just paying him for good measure.

"You're a merciful gal, D," he mutters with an off-colored

tone. The way his voice comes off nauseates me to the memory of our first encounter. *Why the fuck should this sick fuck get to live after what he's put me through? And I'm paying him on top of that. Fuck this.*

I immediately smash the bag of scopolamine into his face. He coughs violently and struggles to fight the drug. Dustin desperately swings his arms out. I pull away, dodging his long finger-nailed swipes as the drug hijacks his frontal cortex and floods his nervous system. *Too much of this shit is like anthrax. It's too much for him to survive.* His jabs dissipate while he foams at the mouth and goes into cardiac arrest. I stand over him as he collapses and watch him seize on the floor to his death.

It takes quite a few hours of processing before realizing that I just so happen to be the constant in nearly every situation. My pain has truly become my strength, and each near-death experience that failed to take me has taught me one thing: *never allow a man to be in the way… Period.*

My mother awakes the following morning to the rotting smell of *criminal carcasses* in the living room. It takes her a moment to realize she's not in American Falls anymore, and she begins to cry. I console her and explain the nature of what has happened.

"It's a miracle either of us are even alive," I tell her on the Porsche ride after she's had time to endure the sight of my dead enemies upon our departure. We have breakfast on the Quintana Roo pier at a high-end restaurant, not far from yesterday's events. It's as if the community is so used to people being killed in plain sight that they seem to just go on with their lives like nothing happened. *Just another news story for Telemundo.*

I order the finest food on the menu, as well as a few drinks in order to keep her from losing it altogether.

Though, she hardly touches her meal. It's a tough conversation explaining to my mother that all means of legitimate earning have been a lie. I tell her the truth. *That I'm an escort who chose to stay in the game long after I could have gotten out.* I explain everything to her over breakfast. She's at a loss for words and manages to finish her drink in two extraneous gulps.

"Devil's Breath?" she asks, not at all considerate of the exact power this drug bestows.

"In the states, it's called scopolamine. Cartels use it to jack wealthy folks free will and short-term memory to have them coherently sign over property deeds, titles, inheritance money, etc. It was used on you by my ex. That's why you're in Mexico with no recollection as to how," I explain.

"Jesus Christ, Domenica, this sounds like a load of horse shit," she replies.

"Tell me how you wound up here, then," I pry, not really wanting to stress her out. *She's clearly attempting to block the trauma by drinking.* My mom breaks down as she struggles to formulate any viable memory prior to being dosed.

"I don't know," she says while sobbing.

"Do you even remember leaving the apartment this morning?" I ask. She apathetically nods, trying to regain her composure.

"Just go easy. I don't know how long the memory synapses take to repair in the brain. I'll find you a doctor first thing."

"I thought when you got sober you gave up your days of messing with shady people?" she scoffs, wiping the tears from her eyes.

"It was a way for me to earn. I didn't see it as a problem until it became fucking dangerous."

"You didn't see drugging rich men for their money as a problem? Where the fuck did I go wrong in raising you?" my mom asks before ordering another cocktail. "Dos mas por favor," she murmurs, exercising her native tongue.

"I saw this as a way to solve my financial ruin. And in all fairness, yours as well."

"Justify it all you want, D. But I've never advocated your path whatsoever," she fires back with a rageful undertone.

"I didn't say I'm proud of my shit. It's just what the fuck I know how to do."

"If you think drugging people and promiscuity is all you're capable of, then I failed you as a parent," she says while practically drowning in her next cocktail.

"This has nothing to do with your parenting. I accept my actions, and I'm accountable for my choices."

"You're a fucking degenerate, Domenica."

"Say it again, mom. For the cheap seats," I reply, throwing three hundred dollars on the table as I stand to get some air on the pier. It takes several minutes before I regain the equanimity to go back to the fucking table.

By the time I get back, my mom is totally blotto. I pour out the last drink she's nursing into the empty water glass, then get in another fight with her on the way back to the Porsche.

"Where the hell are we going now?" she asks with a lavish slur, struggling to put her seatbelt on in a drunken fit.

"Take a nap," I murmur, half wishing I would have taken her to a doctor before going to lunch. I pull up to a bay of satellite payphones on the pier. I scour a large phone directory attached to one of the satellite phones and find the address with mapped directions from the pier to a private jet hangar on the beach.

The signage on the ad reads: *"TOURISTAS Y BONITAS! BIENVENIDOS! PRIVADO JET EXCURSIONS CON JAVIER MENDOZA! DEL MAR CARRIBENO AL OCEAN PACIFICO! VUELA BUENOS AIRES Y COLOMBIA TAMBIAN!"*

I rip the page out of the directory and follow the directions south. I arrive at a gated bay of private hangars in the Porsche and ask the gate attendant for pricing on chartering a jet to Colombia. The attendant has no idea about such an extravagant request. He buzzes me in and directs me to park outside the third hangar to meet a guy who does this sort of thing. I leave my drunk mother in the car and head inside with the air mattress bag full of cash.

The pilot doing maintenance under his private G4 sees me enter the wide-open hangar doors out of the corner of his eye. He rolls out on his work dolly and stands up to see what I'm all about. "Como puedo ayudarte, senorita?" he asks with a polite tone.

"Hablas ingles?" I ask.

He nods while fixing his glasses and wipes a bead of sweat from his lenses. He sets his socket wrench down on the workbench.

"I'm in need of a ride. Name's D," I say, offering my hand out for him to shake.

"Mucho Gusto, D. Me llamo Javier Mendoza," he says while shaking my hand.

"You do charters to Bogota?"

"Not usually. Pero depende dia," he replies, surveying the drunken state of my mother in the Porsche.

"I'm looking to fly today. Does this thing even run?" I ask, referencing the torn-out bottom of his G4.

"May I suggest Air Colombia? I hear they have an excellent first-class feature selection, with the finest ginger ale whiskey infusion to date. You must indulge," Javier insists with a naïvely dismissive tone.

"I prefer to fly private," I reply.

"But public is so much more affordable," he says, trying to make the best of his English dialect.

"Do you want to make money, or not?" I put forth the question bluntly.

"I don't think you can afford what I charge for a roundtrip to Colombia."

"Forty grand each way sound feasible?" I ask, countering his pessimistic prejudgment by tilting the inflatable mattress bag forward so he can see the eighty thousand I set aside in cash. His mannerisms change altogether, and a giant smile comes across his face as if he's won the lottery.

"Will you be needing a parking space for your Porscha?" Javier asks.

"Yep," I reply. "We'll be gone for about a week."

"Pull the Porscha into the hangar and help yourself to the complimentary mini-bar in my office. If you need a little cocaine or amphetamine to wake up, tu amigita, I have a bag in the top drawer of my desk. Take off is in an hour," he says while grabbing his socket wrench and going back to work. A genuine smile makes its way across my face as that familiar return of financial prowess culminates.

DESCANSO

There is nothing more fashionable than flying private over the Costa Rican rainforest wearing complimentary Ray-Bans—except, of course, when cocaine, caviar, and champagne are involved. The side dishes my mother indulges in are compliments of our ghetto-laden G4 pilot, Javier Mendoza.

This behavior is extremely out of character for her. It's as if she suffered severe synapse trauma from the prior week's heavy dosage of scopolamine. It somehow rewired her maternal mind-frame back to her teenage years. Though she always hated drugs when I was battling my addiction.

Oh, how the tables have turned. My mother clearly doesn't want to process the not-so-shocking news that I'm a professional fuck up. I don't take part in any of these chemicals, but I watch resentfully as she downs another glass of bubbly. She spills a trickle of champagne fizz on the posh G4 seat covers as we hit a turbulent air pocket.

"Will you slow the fuck down?" I beckon, stopping her from pouring more coke out of the bag onto the foldup tray table.

"Maybe you're not the only one turning over a new leaf, Domenica."

"You need to take it easy," I reply with a feckless tone.

"Says my escort daughter." She laughs like someone else entirely. I've never seen her so emotionally out of sorts. I snatch the glass, pour the remaining champagne onto the coke bag, and wipe the cellophane coke-smear off the tray table. She gives me a dirty look like I just spoiled her sweet sixteen.

"This is not the fix for your inability to digest the matters at hand. Yes, I'm a prostitute, and yes, you've fallen victim to my choices. I'm sorry for that. But you need to lay the fuck down and get some sleep. It's been a rough couple of weeks for you. It's going to take time to process."

She immediately breaks down as the wayward exhaustion finally sets in. She collapses onto the tray table and delves into the trenches of high-altitude detox.

"She doesn't like the blow or what?" Javier interjects with

a portentous grin, wiping a bead of sweat from his glasses. I shoot him a very discerning *keep your eyes on the sky* look. He quickly shifts his attention back to flying and fixes his glasses so he can better see out the window. Javier yanks back on the yoke in an attempt to ascend above the flock of toucans, but the left engine explodes before he can do so.

"PINCHE TUCANES!" Javier screams as we abruptly descend.

"Did you just hit a fucking bird?" I ask, resentful I gave such a gratuitous bag of cash up-front.

Javier curses, wiping another bead of sweat from his glasses as he pulls back on the yoke. The left engine is practically a giant fireball. My mother panics as I take my sunglasses off to get a better look out the window. Javier does everything in his power not to crash, but we go down hard despite his intentions to salvage the jet.

Jet pilot Javier secures a very unpleasant water landing onto the coastline of the Caribbean, adjacent to the rainforest. A coral boulder brings the G4 to an abrupt stop, crashing through the cockpit and killing Javier instantly. My mother's sobs worsen as I grab her hand and pull out of her fuckin' seat.

I'm more pissed off than anything as the cabin fills with algae-infused seawater. I grab the bag of damp cash next to Javier's crushed body on the floor and drag my mother out through the cockpit. We climb over the boulder, scraping our legs on the way up.

A ten-foot swell barrels over the coral boulder, knocking the bag of cash out of my grip. Both my mother and I are hurled into the ocean as well. I struggle to catch a breath of air as the current rips me from my mother's eye line.

I'm able to pop my head up for a moment before another wave submerges over the top. I can vaguely see the damp mattress bag floating a few meters away. I reach out to grab it, but I'm interrupted by another wave crashing over the coral, drenching the contents of the bag entirely. My mother swims for the beach as I'm caught in a desperate attempt to retrieve a wet ten-thousand-dollar band of cash floating within reach. I desperately snatch the band before being submerged. I grip the money tightly as another swell crashes over my head. Luckily the force of the wave sends my body crashing against the sandy coastline next to my mother.

I struggle to get to my feet before collapsing, furious my money is drowning in the abyss of watery nothingness. My mother coughs up water as the jet sinks into the shallow surges. The cash churns in the nefarious ocean swells like a lottery ticket in a washing machine. The sight is almost too painful to witness with yet another dead body in my wake.

I drop the soaked ten thousand dollars from my clenched grip and lay my head down in the sand to catch my breath. The notion that I'm practically back to square one sets in. *I'm alive, I can earn again, and I'm the fuck out of Mexico. Not all is lost. I can make ten thousand dollars work for me down here, but I want more.* I get to my feet and wade back into the Caribbean.

"Domenica!" my mother yells as I swim amongst foamy

wave breaks. I grab all the salvageable drenched cash humanly possible before tiring out. Unfortunately, the current pulls me towards the sinking jet. The other engine ignites as the rip tide intensifies, sending rocks and debris into the turbine. I can feel the heat from the explosion on my back while I struggle against the current.

My military training kicks in. I replace panic with calculated thought, and swim diagonally against the death tide, fighting Mother Nature's grip on all fronts. I make it back to the shoreline with a fistful of hundreds and crawl back onto the beach, seemingly unscathed. The salt from the Caribbean reminds me how tore up my fucking knees are as my adrenaline rush subsides.

"What the fuck were you thinking?" my mother asks in her resentful, bitter tone. I hold out the soaked hundred-dollar bills for her to see and set the money on top of the salvageable ten-thousand-dollar cash band. I drop to my knees and count the crinkled cash in full, which only brings our total nest egg up to a survivable eleven thousand dollars.

"I won't die some broke, deported whore," I say in a desperate effort to catch my breath. She shakes her head and watches the ocean engulf the remainder of the fiery jet.

My mother shakes her head through her annoying stream of tears. I shrug with the notion that all will be presumably well, then reach into my pocket to check the status of scopolamine. The bag is completed fucking soaked. I did a good enough job sealing the bag to the point where it's still most likely chemically stable. I pocket the scopolamine bag and cash in my wet jeans, then stand to survey our surroundings. There doesn't appear to be any sort of landmarks in sight.

"We need to keep heading south," I say.

"Jesus Christ, Domenica, what is the point?" she asks.

"Colombia," I reply.

"Is this not enough for you to let it be and start over?" she asks while climbing to her feet.

"It's not about money, mom."

"Oh, really? What's it about then? Because it seems to me, you'll do just about anything to get more," she snaps with a nasty tone.

"I have an extremely capable enemy still out there who wants me dead. You think it's wise to hide in some Latin American country and pray they don't find us?" I scoff at her inability to handle what needs to be done.

"Justify things all you want, mija. These people are the fucking cartel, no? What chance do we have against them?" she asks, attempting to put things in perspective.

"Zero if we stay here to rot. Diego knows I'm alive. I can't look over my shoulder the rest of my life."

"Hiding is better than dying. They have an army; you just have your mother," she says, not at all remotely savvy to their technological capability, or mine for that matter.

"Hiding doesn't work."

"Neither will flying down to Colombia and blindly ambushing a bunch of armed thugs."

"That's not the plan."

"So, what then?" she asks, furthermore pissing me the fuck off.

"I'm going to use their product against them," I say.

"How?"she asks, surveying my off-the-cusp reaction.

"By synthesizing an airborne version of scopolamine and using Diego's crew against him," I explain, speculating on the actual feasibility of this idea. My mother is at a loss for words—probably because I'm showing her a side she doesn't recognize or like.

We set up camp on the beach, spending about four hours collecting branches from the rainforest in hopes of setting up a small A-frame shelter. *We get it done by about dusk. Stable enough to suffice for at least the night.* I'm somewhat impressed with my ability not to let the elements fucking depress me.

It's too hot to even consider starting a fire, but the mosquitos are no joke. They seem to come out of the woodwork around dusk. Twenty or thirty of them in hordes the size of wasps. *Nasty fucking parasites.*

I toss and turn all night, unable to procure a proper night's rest. The forest seems to come alive. The ground crawls with ants and all sorts of unverifiable insects, which prevents either of us from sleeping a wink. My mother complains the entire night and cries four times, almost as if you would think she came from a silver spoon.

"GOD DAMNIT!" she yells, standing up in a fit of rage. The moonlight reflects off the A-frame mother-daughter survival hut quite nicely, producing a clear view of the waves rolling off the Caribbean rocks. She smacks a giant crab off her leg. It scurries into the sand and buries itself beneath a rock. The rest of the night isn't any better. We get an early start, leave the A-frame as is, and collect a few bananas from a nearby tree for nourishment. The rain starts to drizzle on us during our journey down the South American coastline. The wildlife is magnificent, but the rain intensifies, and the humidity is horrendous.

"We don't have to worry about going without water," I murmur, trying to shift the perspective into the positive while collecting precipitation off a leaf. We both stop for a moment to hydrate. It doesn't occur to me until later that the leaves we're drinking from could be extremely poisonous. Though at first glance, you wouldn't think so.

After a few rough days of trekking down the coastline, we stumble upon a wooden structure in the trees. The sound of tourist chatter intensifies as we draw nearer. Hidden behind the branches is a decadent balcony with four people having cocktails overlooking the Caribbean Sea. *Jesus Christ, is this a mirage?*

The people look down at my mother and me in the trees. One of them spills her drink, most likely startled by the horrific sight of our woodsy appearance. My mother begins crying again. I roll my eyes, annoyed at her constant need to break down in tears for no apparent reason.

"Ayudamos!" I yell with a tone of urgency. The tourists and resort staff come down right away to see what the hell is going on. I allow my mom to explain the situation through her tearful muddled speech. Her Spanish is much more proficient than mine. They comp us a room for the night and keep insisting on calling emergency services. I have my mother explain that they cannot do so under any circumstances—that it is, in fact, extremely dangerous for us to be on any sort of books or news outlet stories for that matter. I pay them off to keep their mouths shut. *A handsome three hundred dollars per each member of management, plus two hundred for the room service guy procuring ibuprofen and high-end carne asada.*

We chill for three days and do nothing but eat and sleep. I buy a fresh set of clothes in the gift shop and book her a ticket back to the United States so she can get the fuck out of this tropical hell.

The ticket costs a thousand dollars cash at the Santamaria International airport. Without a passport, they're going to keep her in holding where she's safe. I tell her to have the border agents get ahold of Belinsky in Langley as her verification phone call. I write down exactly what she needs to say in order to make it across and give her a hug before taking a cab back to the Almonds and Corals Resort.

I ask a member of the resort management staff for the most direct way to get to Colombia untraced. He puts me in touch with a snakehead immigrant trafficker at some knock-off Verizon store.

I meet the snakehead at the kiosk inside and give him a thousand bucks up-front. His lack of enthusiasm regarding cash reminds me of an old Buddhist I met in the program who taught me that *money is just a tool to hinder or aid us along our spiritual journeys.*

He counts the cash, fixes his baseball cap, and brings me into the cell phone stock room with a few other Chinese immigrants who are counterfeiting iPhones. One of them uses an inkjet laser to whittle a small X on the back of an iPhone 7.

"Usually, people want to go up, not down," the snakehead says with a flippant air of sincerity.

"There will come a time where that's relevant for my situation. As of now, that doesn't happen to be the case," I reply.

"How is your Spanish?" the snakehead asks, stroking his goatee.

"Not where I want it to be."

"Ah, see Farc have ways of getting you in—but border is really tricky this time of year. You have to be fluent to follow instruction."

"I thought you were going to take me?" I infer, pissed my thousand dollars is being used for Chinese brainstorming instead of concrete methodology.

"How are you with tiny spaces?" the snakehead asks,

ignoring my comment altogether.

"Define tiny, Chink Lee… 'Cause I ain't droppin' a G on some bullshit coagulated thought processing. I thought you had a solid way in," I reply, flying off the handle. *I forget how upright the Chinese can be. The look he gives me is damn near despicable.*

"There's no need for that sort of talk," the snakehead replies.

"Well, what the fuck good is my thousand bucks if you don't even know what you're doing?"

"Consultation fee. You don't like it you can get out-my store."

"I'm not paying you for a consultation fee. I'm paying you to have your shit together so I can get into Colombia off the books."

"Expect me to drive you through Panama in Jeep Cherokee like Peruvian tour guide? Not gonna happen. No, sir. Border police take you to jail. Torture, maybe rape. Sell you to cartel and make you full-time street puppet. Want that life? No, sir."

"Chill," I curtly respond.

"Hou's job is to discover best way to get you in, untraced. That's what I do. Give me attitude—I give you nothing."

"My attitude is a lack of patience for poor planning—"

"Respect is what must be learned. Only then, I give you the way—Mingue?" the snakehead clarifies with a heavy Chinese accent. A few of the immigrants counterfeiting phones shoot me an anticipated dirty look.

I bow my head to acknowledge his bullshit, doing everything in my power to refrain from rolling my eyes. He paces over to one of the immigrants and mutters something in Chinese. They speak for a few moments, then shift their attention back to me.

"Cabinas Kaniki has a shipping container we'll fit you in. Must be okay with sulfur dioxide fumes and three-day boat ride," Hou explains.

"Who's going to ensure that I get out when the container docks in Colombia?"

"Dual citizen on other side, Chin-Lee. He runs Cabinas Kaniki shipping channel from Colombia to Costa Rica. Primetime produce exporter. His guys unload empty containers to refill banana boat. Your container will be checked off. Fruit go up, money come down. Border agents look other way. You pay other thousand when he opens container."

"How far is this from Bogota?" I ask, trying to gauge where the fuck I'm going to be.

"Bocas Del Atrato maybe three hundred miles from Bogota. Chin-Lee don't do transport there. He stays on dock all day. Work clean. No fuddy-duddy Bogota business."

"You consider smuggling *people* a clean business?" I ask, shooting him a *don't justify this shit* look. He groans in an over-accentuated manner and mutters something in Mandarin to one of his immigrant affiliates building an iPhone. His affiliate replies in Mandarin while staring me down.

"Come now. We go," Hou says, yanking my arm as he pulls me across the room. We head outside through the bustling crowd of Costa Rican natives to his Mitsubishi Eclipse parallel parked between two vans. He opens the door for me on the passenger's side and mutters something in a heavy Mandarin accent. I interpret his gibberish as: *get in the car, bitch,* then do so accordingly. I close the door as he crosses back around and finds his way to the driver's seat.

Hou starts his vehicle and backs out of the parallel parking spot with meticulous timing. He pulls forward into traffic and drives towards the Caribbean coastline.

"What business you have in Colombia?" Hou asks.

"Nunya," I reply.

"Nun-huh?" he asks. I can't help but let out a brief nauseated chuckle. Clearly, this man's English is not on the up-and-up. Hou furrows his brow while driving through traffic and shoots me an inquisitive glance.

"It's an American expression," I briefly explain.

"What does it mean?" Hou asks, not at all a fan of me making light of his language barrier.

"It means our business is between us, and mine is not for you to know at all."

"Be careful. Chin-Lee won't smuggle you back if you have cargo. He doesn't mess with Colombian way," Hou warns.

"His services are only required by me for entry," I vaguely state.

"You have contacts there?" Hou asks, stroking his goatee as if he's contemplating on trying to broaden his horizons.

"You ask a hell of a lot of questions for a fuckin' snakehead," I snap at him in an attempt to back Hou the fuck off.

He nods and refocuses his attention on the road. We approach the Cabinas Kaniki shipping port with caution. Several Costa Rican natives unload a small ship with two large CONEX containers full of limes and bananas. A Chinese snakehead with a pompadour haircut sprays the produce with sulfur dioxide, causing a cluster of yellow banana spiders to flee from their death out of the produce.

Hundreds of spiders slow to a crawl on the CONEX floor and gradually die on the docks as they try to escape. The pompadour sheik Chinaman goes a little too heavy, drenching the fruit in a full coating of pure Costa Rican preservative.

"Esta Mucho! No Mas!" a Hispanic crew member yells at the Chinaman. The Chinaman ignores him and continues to spray the soaked produce, using the language barrier as his ace in the hole to keep spraying. One of the Costa Rican crew guys displays his wet freight glove to the Chinaman to show how overindulgent this spray job really is. The Chinaman couldn't give a fuck. He lights a cigarette and continues, treating the Costa Ricans like second class citizens.

Hou rushes out of the car and stops him from spraying. The Chinaman listens to Hou, at first glance out of respect. They talk for a few moments, then direct their attention towards me in the Mitsubishi.

It takes a few moments for the introduction to happen, and it all goes down in the Mitsubishi Eclipse. The pompadour-enthusiast Chinaman tells me to come back tonight around 9 PM. That's when the crates and docks will be empty. Hou and I share an afternoon of awkward coffee conversation at a place called *Cafe De Chino*.

The restaurant is a strange combo of overweight Costa Rican's and black-market Chinese snakeheads indulging in a merged enjoyment of fresh roast. We discuss more than I'd like in order to kill time, then he proposes to drop me off an hour early. I offer to buy dinner to keep the arrival time on point.

He agrees, then we eat. At 8:45 Costa Rican time, Hou escorts me back to the Cabinas Kaniki Shipping docks. I meet the Chinaman rocking the pompadour outside of the Mitsubishi. They take a moment to scan the immediate area to make sure it's clear before I climb into the container.

Prospects appear safe, and the docks are empty. Hou and the Chinaman covertly escort me into an empty shipping container. Hou grabs heavy padlock out of the Mitsubishi to secure the hinged doors of the CONEX. He loads a few cases of water in the Connex along with some ramen noodles and hot dogs.

The Chinaman loads a generator inside the CONEX with a lamp, electric blanket, and a hibachi grill. It's quite spacious. They go out of their way to make sure I'm comfortable during this sketchy endeavor.

"Boat leave early morning. You stay in all night. Eat, sleep, relax. Make noodle. You have-use bathroom, squat in corner—spray sulfur dioxide to kill smell. Do same for pee. Chin-Lee see you in three day," Hou explains as he steps out of the connex. The fact that they're comfortable with me defecating in a banana boat tells me everything I need to know about how they handle business. I nod as he shoots me a wink and closes the door.

It takes roughly five hours from the time Hou locks the CONEX to the moment I feel the boat depart. The ride is cumbersome with wave knocks as we leave the port, nauseating me to the point of dry heaving.

A few hours into the ride, my hunger sets in. I fasten the propane tank to the Hibachi to cook myself a package of dry ramen. The grill is instantly knocked on its side from the ocean sway. It takes several attempts before I develop a semi-successful cook-eat-sleep routine. I use tepid boiled seawater from the CONEX floor to cook my ramen until evaporation. If anything, it just makes the noodles a bit saltier. They say not to ingest salt-water, but I've never heard anything taboo about cooking with it.

I use the corner to tend to my bathroom duties and refrain from covering it up with sulfur dioxide in close confinements. I'm aware of the damage this chemical does to a person's lungs in such conditions.

One must think Chin-Lee will give the banana boat a good spray down after I dock. It really makes me question the quality of produce that is shipped to the United States. Proletarian ambition almost always equals criminal means of export.

On day three, I encounter what feels like an abrupt stop. Though it's hard to tell if that signifies the Conex has docked because there are no windows. I catch the grill as it falls and look towards the door in hopes of any sign of outside handling.

ORGANIZED CHAOS

Amongst the humidity, I find a modicum of peace in knowing that I'm one step closer to ridding my enemies off the face of the planet. I know the hell I've walked through is nothing in comparison to the paradise I will experience when I have the cash to carry out my will.

It's a dark sentiment to think murder provides damnation to one and tranquility to another. The ripple effect of how selling your soul earns you copious amounts of cheddar is unparalleled. I think the worst part about criminality is the unknown ailments of the human mind. The darkest corners of my soul are now illuminated to do one thing.

I've never considered such horrendous acts as a necessity until my life was in complete danger. Peace of mind is worth more to me now than ever before, and there are no lengths I won't go through to ensure harmony fucking happens. Tricks used to call me crazy when I was high, but sobriety has put a whole new spin on what calculated madness really is. The dismissiveness that humans give to the reputation of prostitutes is despicable. Perhaps that's why I hate men so much. It's not that I don't like their money; it's that they perceive me to be this weak little Mexican chick.

That persona gets old. I try to act as justified as possible, but this condemned prospect makes it hard to refrain from going batshit.

The stares I get from Chin-Lee and his crew as they open the CONEX is beyond despicable. It's disheartening to think they view my close quarters as sloppy. A few of them make comments in Mandarin while laughing. I can't understand what they're saying, but I comprehend the tone quite well.

I pull a thousand dollars out of my jeans and display the bills in plain sight.

"What's so funny you can't say to my face in English?" I ask with a furious tenor.

"What's funny is you pay a thousand dollars to come to the world's finest shithole instead of using that money to get out of South America. You're obviously not a coke mule. What could be so important that an American girl like yourself has to be in such terrible confinements to travel South?" Chin-Lee asks.

"None of your goddamn business," I reply.

"These are my docks. It's absolutely my business," Chin-Lee clarifies.

"I have enemies," I murmur, shoving the stack into his hand.

"Enemies?" he asks while counting the cash and handing a few hundreds to his guys. I nod as I climb out of the CONEX and plant my feet firmly on the rotted dock.

"Guys who want me dead," I murmur.

"Which cartel did you piss off?" he asks, ignoring my need for discretion.

"Specifics aren't your concern. I suggest you thank me for the cash and let me pass without further question," I briefly elaborate, furious these chink fucks have the audacity to be so goddamn nosey. Chin-Lee shares a look of joy with his crew and steps aside, almost as if he enjoys a tiny woman with a vulgar mouth.

I fix my hair and proceed to pass unscathed. One of them says something in Mandarin, and the rest cackle behind me while I walk away.

I head towards a dirt road off the docks and hitchhike my way to the closest tavern I can find. The vibe is not touristy at all. In fact, it's rather jungle-esq. Mostly people from the shipping trade it appears. Chin-Lee enters the bar and sits on the stool next to me.

"You following me?" I ask.

"You shouldn't be here," Chin-Lee iterates while throwing twenty bucks down to order himself a drink.

"I'll give you half your wad back to turn around."

"Aww, half? How generous of you." I say while munching

down on a piece of ice from my Colombian triple-decker Martini.

"A fine piece of American ass doesn't belong in a port like this. You're going to get abducted, especially if you hang around these environments," Chin-Lee explains, clearly expressing genuine concern for my wellbeing.

"Kind of you to enlighten me on how terrifying this atmosphere is. However, I just came from the taint of Mexico—dealt with a much worse class of people. Thank you very much."

"Same class of people, butter-bump. I'm telling you you're barking up the wrong jungle."

"What cajones you have to even be associated with a gal like me."

"If you're on that big of a Colombian shit list, your only option is to get out of dodge."

"Get the fuck out of my face, or I'll throw my drink in yours."

Chin-Lee processes my dismissive tone with a weak shrug. He stands from the barstool and shakes his head, carrying his drink with him on the way out. Chin-Lee ambitiously finishes half his cocktail before reaching the door. He gives me a quarter-ass, two-finger salute on the way out and leaves me to wander through the abyss of drunk jungle fever. I find myself dazed after the second drink, fucking around too much with the 1980s arborvitae-covered jukebox. I'm drawing too much attention to myself. *Who gives a shit? Nobody here is connected to the guy who wants me dead in this shithole jungle bar.*

I flash my smile to a cholito with a handlebar mustache and share a couple dances with him near the barstool. Hotel California plays by the Gypsy Kings—the Spanish version is not nearly as classic as The Eagles original. The Colombians in the bar take notice of my staggered looseness and smile in hopes they might get lucky. I settle with the bartender and ask the guy with the handlebar mustache for a ride to the nearest town.

He gives me a ride to some low-level swamp hotel in Chaja, Colombia. It's an uncomfortable, twenty-minute motorcycle ride through the third world carved out dirt road into the jungle marsh. I give the guy with a handlebar mustache an unprotected blowjob in the parking lot in exchange for his services, then send him away with a temperamental look after he finishes. The cholito nods, awkwardly satisfied, then gets back on his bike and leaves me to check in by myself.

"How many nights you want to stay, senorita?" the front desk guy asks with a mouthful of potato chips. I stare at the questionable chipotle stains on his wife beater v-neck and take a minute to process.

"Um, one is fine."

"Fumar or no?" he asks while picking the chip crumbs off his shirt and nonchalantly eating the remnants.

"Nonsmoking is fine," I politely say.

The front desk guy shrugs, finishes eating the crumbs, and then egregiously licks his fingertips. I'm nearly sick to my stomach watching his obese carb-indulgent gestures. He wipes his hands with an already used napkin, then passes me a room key.

"Room 106," he says. I take a moment before grabbing the room key, then do so unwillingly. The bitter feeling of damp hand clamminess sets in as I pocket the key and head down the hall to get settled.

I immediately shower and use the in-room hand sanitizer and tissues to wipe down the keycard. A feeling of calm returns after lying down in the cum stained waterbed. I let sleep meander its way in and rest for what feels like an eternity, though it's only about noon when I awake.

I catch a cab to the nearest public transportation station and buy a one-way bus ticket to Bogota. The ride is long, uncomfortable, and smelly. It reeks of homeless immigrants and mildew-riddled enchiladas. Eight hours later, the bus arrives in downtown Bogota, land of the highest-paid criminals on earth.

The ones who operate in the shadows thrive in such an atmosphere of bustling chaos. It makes me wonder why the economy is so fucked when some of the wealthiest drug lords reside in the foothills. Almost as if the *greed is good* notion blocks the ebb and flow of cash circulation amongst the impoverished. You can feel the sadness within the general population just by studying their faces. They look tired—not necessarily in a physical sense. More so in an emotional erudition from the outbursts of murder over money.

Insatiability is what fuels every human who puts their baseline ethics on the wayside for a glass of champagne and a four-thousand square foot house to play billiards and snort coke in. The fear of lack creates a domino effect in a certain person's mind, which creates voracity in some and complacency in others.

Financial rapaciousness is the driving force separating the debt collectors from its downtrodden citizens. Breaking and bending laws isn't even a justification anymore in the eyes of a man who's had enough defeat. It's a mode of survival to gain supremacy over those who lack the balls to get what they want out of life. Most people in high places had to walk through hell to achieve their ambitions. If attained, they'll stop at nothing to keep the freedom that has been awarded from such heinous trials.

There are eyes in this crowd at the bus stop I recognize. Not on a personal level, but in a general means. The ones far and few between who see the weaknesses in people like I do. Those who can spot vulnerabilities at first glance without hardly any conversation. They wear many modes of attire and come from a place where things were not handed to them.

Game recognizes game on any front, despite current financial status. I can see the difference in those who have this innate sensibility to the ones who just merely exist to survive, trying to escape the warranted wild west autonomy that is Colombia.

From the dealer on the bench to the man in the Armani suit drinking espresso on the adjacent patio. The look in their eyes in the same: watchful, collected, and succinct. The only difference is one surrendered to their environment early on, and the other is in the process of serious financial breakthrough.

Then, of course, you have your upper-middle-class American tourist families walking amongst the rest of the general public. Snapping selfies at the bus stop like they're paying homage to Travel Guide by creating their own 4K Pablo Picassos. They then post the finished result on Instagram for their friends and family to gawk at while their dogs are probably neglected back at home in the United States. *So lame this first world naiveté truly is amongst the undeserved wealth.*

Belinsky grabs my arm before I'm able to cross the street and pulls me into a white suburban with two other off-the-reserve federal agents.

"The fuck are you doing down here?" I ask with utmost rage of his attempted interception.

"Stopping you from getting yourself killed. Got a call from Orquid Delgado at the fuckin airport border in El Paso. Mom was very vocal over the phone about your plans. Raised eyebrows in Langley. My counterintelligence team was extremely adamant about me not stopping you at all so SC could do you without us wasting tax dollars. They fuckin know you're here, D.

"Oh, so you're on their roll now?"

"No, but how's about you slow yours? SC banks a few congressmen in the states who have major FBI sway. One of my superiors included. You're going against the wrong guys."

"You were helping me against them."

"That was before I was briefed on their current standing with my supervisor. Look, I don't want to see a girl get whacked for the wrong reasons. I'm endangering my job by even being here."

"You know what happened with the Afiliados?" I ask.

"I know two of them are dead because of you," Belinsky replies.

"So why the fuck do you even care what I do?"

"Because you aren't afraid to die, lolita. I view that as a problem for a mother who was in tears at the border."

"Don't call me that," I reply.

"I see a lot of me in you. Unfortunately, as much as I would like the world to rid itself of the bad guys, my ethics forbid the heinous shit."

"How'd you get down off the record?" I ask.

"Friends in low places. You?"

"Same."

"You mean tricks in worn out spaces?" Belinsky sneers.

"Fuck you."

"Take a left up here, Ricardo." Belinsky shifts his attention to the driver. Ricardo bangs a hard left down an alley and approaches a dumpster next to a beat-to-shit wooden door.

Ricardo jumps out of the front seat with the other agent and opens the door to the alley corridor. Belinsky grabs my hand and leads me inside a dingy federal safe room. The room has no windows and reeks of cigarette smoke and Jim Beam.

Belinsky pulls a chair out for me to sit. He takes his pistol out of his side holster and hands it to me without any regard for my felonies. I sit down in the chair and check the mag. *Seven rounds.*

"You must seriously be in the fucking lurch to be handing me a gun."

"No more lurch than you, corazon. We're all fuckin targets down here." Ricardo closes the door behind us and sits at the table next to me.

"How much cash you got in your pocket?" Belinsky pries.

"Why?"

"Just answer the question."

"Four grand."

"Give me three of that now. Keep a thousand for when

you land."

"Land where?"

"Oahu," Belinsky says as he shoves a plane ticket and a doctored passport into my left hand. The name on the ticket and ID is *Calista Megarian.* Somehow, the woman in the picture looks identical to me. "Flight departs at Noon today out of Bogota," Belinsky finishes.

"You need to let me do this," I say while standing from my chair. One of the agents makes a hand gesture for me to sit back down.

"No can do, " Belinsky iterates.

"What's one more notch on that tarnished belt gonna do for your moral high ground?"

"Langley needs the scopolamine cartel unscathed for the time being."

"So they can dose up more politicians?"

"Domenica—"

"They took shots at you in Juárez, you stupid fuck."

"Take this as a godsend. You're stepping down.

"No the fuck I'm not."

"You either board this flight in a timely fashion, or Diego has his way with you. It isn't rocket science, sweetheart."

"Are they funding some sort of provision for your supervisor?" I ask.

"They're funding the *shut the fuck up and walk away before it's too late* provision," Belinsky sneers while expecting a reaction from one of the other agents. Neither of them blink. His comment irritates me beyond all else. I hide the fact that I'm furious with a well-endowed smirk.

"Let's go," Belinsky says, turning his back to me as he leads the way out. I abruptly shoot both of his agents in their bulletproof vests while their backs are turned, then press the hot barrel of the pistol to Belinsky's neck. I grip the nape of his bulletproof vest as he lowers his M4 in shock, watching the agents crawl towards their weapons on the floor.

"You either take me take me to Diego, or I do you right here, you sick fuck," I say in a very non-bullshit tone.

I shoot a golf ball size hole through Ricardo's hand as he reaches for his M4, then pump a round into the other agent's head. I push Belinsky through the door into the alleyway.

"Calm your fuckin shit," Belinsky yells in a taken aback tone.

"You're taking me," I demand, grabbing the keys from Ricardo's pocket as I dip back inside to finish him off. Blood splatters all over my shoes from the chunks of brain matter split through his skull.

"A whore and a fed verse a hundred-man army is slim-to-no odds, you fuckin cunt. Diego's compound is gated, and he's got surveillance all over his street," Belinsky yells with his M4 pointed at my head.

"Surveillance is your M.O.," I snap, raising my gun back his face. "You really gonna kill me?" I ask.

"You just clipped two of my guys and got four Gs in cash. Seems like a viable option at this point."

"Prying this cash from my hands might prove sort of difficult considering I follow suit if you pump me full of lead," I say, furious he won't listen.

"Why is this individual so goddamn important for you to kill?"

"That's none of your concern," I snap, furious at his attempted reasoning.

"And what's your part in all of this, Domenica? Blameless victim caught up in a whorish quandary working for the wrong people—"

Before he's able to finish his sentence, I shoot him in the bulletproof vest four times, knocking him completely unconscious as he drops his gun and hits his head on the rearview mirror of the SUV.

I remove Belinsky's bulletproof vest and put it on as he staggers back to consciousness. I force him into the passenger's seat and snatch the handcuffs from his belt. I cuff him to the door grip as he grabs his ribcage in agony.

"Don't ever fucking call me a whore again."

"You're not going to make it out of this, you fucking cunt," Belinsky says, barely able to catch his breath.

BLOOD-CURDLING DARKNESS

There's no feeling more liberating than driving through the streets of Colombia in a federal-grade SUV. The armored windshield is not only an additive to my pursuit of vengeance but an assurance that this fucking rig will hold up if I decide to use it as a battering ram.

Diego is one of the most capable people south of the border, hands down. It terrifies me to think he knows I'm coming. However, there's something to be said about his lack of effort in trusting his crew to handle his dirty work for him. It's the only reason I'm still alive. A crew of any kind can be faulty, especially when they're juggling their own wants and desires on top of carrying out their boss's orders.

The biggest pitfall with kingpins is their inability to stay in touch with the street shit that made them number one in the first place. If money is the goal above all else, maintaining it should be of no lesser importance than it was to achieve it.

Wealth seems to bring about a tendency to kick back among those who achieve it fast—allowing the underdogs to come up and eventually take out those who have it. There's always someone riding under the *come up* in search of weaknesses no matter how good the settling pay is.

Everyone wants to be number one, period. It's a catch twenty-two of a mind-fuck, which is probably why Belinsky snatched me up so quickly. His intentions are to save me from myself—or whatever cosmic bullshit he thinks he's doing. *But he's just in my way. Plain and simple.* I can't afford any more roadblocks. Despite my justifications, I'm forced to reckon with my part in all of this.

I take a left on Calle Modesto while pointing the M4 at Belinsky's Adam's apple.

"Not much use without your Kevlar, are you?" I fruitfully antagonize.

"I'm not telling you where the scope house is."

"Then I'll call your superior and get it myself after I put a bullet in your throat."

"You make that call, and you'll be instantly marked. Then it'll just be you against them with three dead agents on your conscience."

"Ha," I curtly respond.

"You're out of your mind, you crazy cunt," Belinsky mumbles under his breath.

"The directions, Belinsky," I impatiently beckon.

"Uncuff me, and I'll tell you," Belinsky says. He tries to negotiate his way out of the handcuffs with a weak attempt to convince me our chances of survival go up if he's armed. I call his bluff and reiterate his zero-leverage factor. Belinsky finally believes I'll shoot him and starts navigating me through the city to buy time for himself. I can't tell if he's full of shit or not as far as the directions he's provided.

We reach a road going up a narrow hill through the seemingly wealthier neighborhoods. "Take a left," Belinsky utters as we approach a Colombian suburban intersection.

I take a left onto Calle Tracindo and maneuver my way around parked cars up the narrow dirt road.

We drive for several minutes before the road begins to widen out into a dense jungle dirt road at the top of the hill. An armored black Escalade swerves out of a ditch and cuts in front of our SUV to slow us down. I attempt to swerve around the Escalade and pick up speed, but the guy driving the Escalade blocks me in.

"Who the fuck is this prick?" I ask rhetorically, full well knowing it's probably one of Diego's lookouts.

"I'm not going to die at the hands of a whore. Uncuff me right fuckin now!" Belinsky says, furious he's lost all power in this situation. I ram the back bumper of the Escalade and roll my window down.

I stick the M4 out the window and grip the stock tight for the impending recoil. Using one hand, I squeeze off several rounds into the back windshield of the Escalade, killing the driver instantly. The Escalade abruptly spirals into a nearby ditch on the right side of the road.

I swerve around the immobilized vehicle and lead-foot the gas pedal while rolling the window back up. Belinsky has an *oh shit* look on his face like I've never seen before. An enormous estate comes into view up ahead. A massive gate blocks the surrounding compound. Four guards stand ready outside. They point their machine guns at me as if they knew I was coming.

I run over the estate guards at the end of the dirt road, driving past the open gate without much resistance. The scopolamine house is busier than I remember. Several Mexicans and Colombians are out front, expecting my arrival with fully automatic weapons.

I'm greeted with several shots to the front of the SUV. The bulletproof glass does its job, saving both our lives. Many guards are killed by my reckless pursuit of not giving a fuck. I run them over without regret.

I crash the SUV in the living room of the scopolamine house. White powder and cash submerge the hood of the vehicle. I stop myself from getting out of the SUV, fully aware of the toxic risk breathing in that horrific powder. I stick the M4 out of the firing hole in the driver's side door as the scopolamine nearly doses everyone in the house, sending several guards into cardiac arrest.

"DON'T!" Belinsky begs as I unload several rounds into the chemists already inhaling tampered air.

Several armed men fire rounds at the vehicle. They drop to their knees from the hazmat dose of scopolamine flooding their central nervous systems. The airborne chemical begins to shut their bodies down as many of them go into cardiac arrest.

I quickly shift the SUV in reverse and back out of the living room, running several more non-dosed guards over. Unfortunately, it's too late. The scopolamine has already entered the air vents of the SUV. I can feel the harshness of this chemical entering my lungs. My head begins to spin. I look over at Belinsky, going into cardiac arrest from the airborne chemical dose.

This is it. It must be. Several guards outside swarm the car and fire their semi-automatic machine guns at our vehicle. The glass breaks as several bullets hit Belinsky, killing him instantly. I feel sharp pains in my chest as I'm hit with their ammo.

I look down—a few of the bullets have made it through the Kevlar. The amount of blood is unfathomable, and my stomach is emaciated beyond recognition. This is the end. I never deserved a life where I get what I want. *If only I walked away from that first hit. If only I had done things differently.*

The cathartic restitution in knowing that I at least killed Aemilian resonates as more bullets penetrate the vest. I drift out of consciousness, feeling completely numb, and fade into blood-curdling darkness.

UNCONVENTIONAL KINSHIP

I awake several hours later with a breathing tube jammed down my throat. A suited Colombian man stands over the table. He looks down at me with a horrific gaze. He lights up a cigarette and gently inhales the toxic fumes. He aggressively blows the smoke into my face. I'm forced to inhale without much of a choice.

"Do you know where you are right now?" the man asks. I'm unable to respond. I use everything in my power to shake my head, but I can't even do that.

"You're at Jesús Malverde Hospital in Bogotá. You've been shot three times in the stomach." The man inhales another puff of smoke and blows it back in my face. My eyes begin to water from the proximity. I tear rolls down my left cheek as I watch this man pace back and forth.

"You're paralyzed, Domenica. Most assuredly, it would be impossible for you to make a full recovery given your condition. I put you on life support because I wanted you to die by my hands, not my security team's. That tube is feeding oxygen into your lungs. If I turn it off, you will die. That would be too courteous for your iniquities."

I try to scream, but nothing comes out. It's like I'm stuck in a horrendous nightmare. *Could this be happening?*

"Do you know who I am?" he asks rhetorically.

Sandello, I think to myself.

"Your biological father," he says without flinching.

The man grips onto the breathing tube and jams it violently down my throat as if he's snaking a drainpipe. I struggle to gasp for air, but nothing comes out. I can feel the lining of my esophagus rupture. He brutally continues until I lose consciousness.

ABOUT THE AUTHOR

From the age of ten, Alyx Gaudio was a natural-born storyteller. He made an array of short films with his friends and posted them on YouTube. When Alyx finally saved up enough money to live in Los Angeles, he was rejected by almost every new-talent development agent in town. He managed to land a few small rolls by self-submitting and crashing auditions.

His first on-set role was the Disney Channel Movie, *Dadnapped*, which got him his Screen Actors Guild Card. The same year he booked a supporting role in the feature film *Justin Time*.

With these IMDB credits, Gaudio was ready to land solid representation. Unfortunately, this wasn't as easy as it appeared. After eight arduous years of working nightclubs in Southern California, he moved back to his hometown and began to write.

At the age of twenty-seven, Gaudio completed his first book and self-published on Amazon. *Borrachero* gained critical acclaim in the indie world and paved the beginning of a fresh start for the young storyteller. Alyx currently resides in Florida and is working on his third novel.

www.ingramcontent.com/pod-product-compliance
Lightning Source LLC
Chambersburg PA
CBHW020332160726
47992CB00004B/1810